Lock Down Publications and Ca$h
Presents

I0637480

Embracing The Love of a Boss

Written by

Meesha

Copyright © 2024 MEESHA
EMBRACING THE LOVE OF A BOSS

All rights reserved. No part of this book may be reproduced in any
form or by electronic or mechanical means, including information
storage and retrieval systems without permission in writing from the
publisher, except by a reviewer who may quote brief passages in
review.

First Edition 2024

Printed in the United States of America

This is a work of fiction. Names, characters, places, and incidents either
are products of the author's imagination or are used fictitiously. Any
similarity to actual events or locales or persons, living or dead, is
entirely coincidental.

Lock Down Publications
P.O. Box 944
Stockbridge, GA 30281
www.lockdownpublications.com

Like our page on Facebook: Lock Down Publications
www.facebook.com/lockdownpublications.ldp

Stay Connected with Us!

Text **LOCKDOWN** to 22828 to stay up-to-date with new releases, sneak peaks, contests and more…

Like our page on Facebook:
Lock Down Publications

Join Lock Down Publications/The New Era Reading Group

Visit our website:
www.lockdownpublications.com

Follow us on Instagram:
Lock Down Publications

Email Us: We want to hear from you!

Acknowledgements

Book 27! When I started my writing journey, I didn't foresee being able to come up with so many different storylines. It has been a joy for me to pen characters and real-life situations for you all to enjoy. It is because of my loyal readers who have rock with me from the beginning and the ones that gave me a fair chance that has kept me going throughout the years. I want to thank y'all from the bottom of my heart. I love my Ghostreaders so much.

I also want to thank a group of special women who were new to the Ghostwriter but have showed up and showed out this year alone. Jackie, Angie, Cookie, and Krystal. You ladies have held me down and got the word out about the Ghostwriter in just a short time all through Chicago. That's what I'm talking about! All of you are now officially Ghostreaders and I welcome y'all with open arms.

Last but not least, Pen Pusha! Dedra, thank you for everything! You know what it is!

I hope y'all enjoy this book. Of course, it's something different than what you all are accustomed to reading from me. I love y'all so much!

#Iamtheghostwriter

Chapter 1

"How you let a nigga with a slew of bitches break your heart?" Jackie asked bewilderedly as the rays from the sun enhance the color of her eyes. "That's what yo' ass get!"

"See, that's what you *not* gon' do. If I remember correctly, you were the one who set up the blind date; unbeknownst to me. You're the one who should've been spilling Cyrus' dirt being he was your friend from the start. I'm sure you know everything his dirty ass is doing when he's not with me."

Kameeko, known as Koko to her family and friends, was fuming because her best friend of all people was actually belittling her for the situationship she was currently in. Truthfully speaking, Koko didn't know about Cyrus' extracurricular activities until she was knee-deep into their courtship. After years of being loyal, loving on him and making what Koko believed were memorable moments, all of his infidelities came out in droves.

Thinking about all the I love you, good morning calls, and texts, Koko's heart was in shambles. One thing she thought was true, Cyrus would be her last love. Oh, how wrong was she. At Twenty-eight years of age, Koko wasn't about to get stuck on a train going nowhere fast. It was bad enough she had been going through the song and dance for years.

"Did you hear anything I just said?" Jackie asked with an attitude.

"No, I didn't. What did you say?"

Rolling her eyes as she bit the tip of the fry she was eating, Jackie huffed before repeating herself. "I asked, what are you going to do? Every time you complain about Cyrus, he spits sweet nothings in your ear and you continue to deal with him and his bullshit."

Koko knew her friend was right, but there was something different about it that day. Koko wanted to be happy and she just wasn't at the point of happiness in her relationship anymore. She was tired of females finding her on social media loving all her posts and laughing in the comments. Koko ignored the pettiness, but inside it made her seethe. She didn't even bring the shit to Cyrus because all he was going to do was deny it 'til he was blue in the face. Koko was waiting for one of them hoes to come to her as a woman so she could eat their asses alive. Jackie thought she was out of the line of fire. Koko realized she hadn't responded to the blame she'd placed upon her.

"I'm done. There's nothing Cyrus can say to make shit right this time. But back to what I said earlier, why didn't you tell me what he was doing behind my back?"

"Just because me and Cyrus are friends doesn't mean I keep up with what he's doing outside of you." Jackie scoffed. "The only reason I know half of the things taking place in y'all relationship is because *you* tell me. Don't make it seem like I'm the one holding out on information because I don't get down like that. You've had years to learn everything there is to know about him. It's time for you to open your eyes to the bullshit you claim to be tired of."

Koko laughed sarcastically because she was fighting the urge to curse Jackie out in the public establishment. Glancing around the room to calm herself, she was going to allow Jackie to have fun with the pain she knew Koko was trying hard to suppress. Sitting at the table quietly picking over her food, Koko's phone vibrated on the table and she glanced at the screen with a scowl on her face. She silenced the call and let it ring until the voicemail picked up. There was never a day gone by that Koko had ever not answered when Cyrus called. There was a first time for everything because she refused to entertain him nor waste a minute of her time talking.

Drama was something Koko didn't partake in. Avoiding confrontation at all costs was something she tried to practice daily. Koko knew addressing the situation was something she would have to do sooner than later. The time was not at the moment because if she was to say something about the text she had received, things wouldn't end well for Cyrus' ass. She wanted to see how long he would act as if nothing was presented to her. Until then, she was going to continue on with life as she saw it because Koko knew, her time was up with the man she loved.

A couple weeks prior, Koko found out about a secret Cyrus had been keeping. His skeletons fell out of the closet when she'd gone to pay him a visit at the Minnesota Correctional Facility in St. Cloud where Cyrus was serving his last week of a six-month sentence. She drove over an hour to see him and was smacked in the face with his infidelities yet again. Holding down a man who constantly cheated at every turn was dumb but that was part of life when love played a major role in the equation. Koko turned a blind eye to the things her man did in the streets; a child was something she refused to overlook.

After signing in and getting searched, Koko sat in an empty chair as she waited for her visit with Cyrus. She opened the Kindle app on her phone so she could finish reading A Thug's Street Princess *by a new-to-her author named Meesha. The book was good as hell. As she was reading, a small hand on her leg caught Koko's attention. There was a little boy no older than a year using her as leverage to stand to his feet. Without thought, Koko reached out for his hand to help him out.*

"Cyrus, get off that woman," his mother said as she walked in our direction.

With her head tilted to the side, the smile fell from Koko's face. She looked at the boy long and hard. Her ears had to be playing tricks on her because there was no way Cyrus had a child. Taking in the little boy's features, it became clear to Koko that he indeed belonged to the man she had been in a relationship with for the past three years. From his cheekbones, the dimples in both of his cheeks, his chocolate complexion, and bowed legs, baby Cyrus looked identical to his father.

"Daddy is going to be so happy to see you trying to walk," the woman said, bringing attention to herself as she smiled down at her child.

Taking in the woman's features, Koko had never seen her before. For clarification, Koko conjured up a conversation with the woman. "He's handsome. How old is he?" she asked.

"He's eleven months and bad as hell. He's definitely his daddy's child. Got his DNA running all through his blood." She laughed, picking the toddler up into her arms. "I'm so glad Big Cyrus will be getting out next week so he'll be there to celebrate his son's first birthday next month."

"How cute. He's a junior," Koko said trying her best to hide the sarcasm in her voice.

"Sure is. Cyrus Latrell Davis, Junior." The mother smiled.

Tears burned Koko's eyes as she excused herself. Crying as she rushed to her vehicle, Koko got inside and drove off. There was no way she would've been able to confront Cyrus at the visit about the child without ending up behind bars herself.

Shaking her head, Koko was brought back to reality when her phone started ringing again. Cyrus called a few more times before he started flooding her text notifications. Reading every one of them, Koko never responded. It was hard not to reply because he was saying everything right at the wrong time. Cyrus was clueless to the things she knew and Koko's silence was speaking louder than any of the words dancing in her head.

"I'm about to head out. I have a major project I need to complete by the end of the week."

"You in your feelings and I understand. Just know I'm here for you no matter the day or the hour," Jackie said, sifting through the bills in her wallet. "Lunch is on me today."

Koko nodded mumbling thank you loud enough for her friend to hear. Gathering her purse, she made sure her keys were in hand as she stood to leave. Jackie couldn't allow Koko to vacate the premises in a saddened mood. Her bluntness always caused a slight rift between them, but they always made up without discussing the problems Koko continuously had with Cyrus.

Jackie met Koko at a salon in North Minneapolis. She knew the quiet woman wasn't from the area and started a conversation with her. From that day the two built a bond and Jackie figured she'd set her up with her homeboy Cyrus. She saw how Cyrus treated the chicken heads he wasn't serious about, but Koko was a different breed. Jackie thought she would be the one to change him into a better man. Had she known he wasn't going to treat Koko right, Jackie wouldn't have even brought the two together.

"Koko, you know I love you and want nothing but the best for you. If Cyrus is who you want to be with, talk to him about what's going on," Jackie said as she rounded the table. "You talk about everything with me and don't make any moves to end the way he treats you. Your heart is already invested and I know it's easier said than done. Don't let him keep playing in your face."

Jackie hadn't said anything Koko hadn't already thought about. The thing about it was, Koko hadn't told her about the child Cyrus had. They were more like brother and sister. There was no way Jackie didn't know about Cyrus junior. Her loyalty was with him, and Koko couldn't be mad because it wasn't Jackie's job to tell her what Cyrus had going on.

She gave Jackie a quick hug and rushed out of the building. The cool air hit Koko in the face just as a lone tear slid down her cheek. All she wanted to do was go to her studio and get lost in what she loved above everything else; her craft.

She opened the door of her 2023 Mercedes Benz GLB 250 she'd gifted herself after winning the top prize on a popular chocolatier show. Koko didn't think she had what it took to go all the way, but with the guidance of *Amaury Guichon* she did just that. She missed the opportunity to lead a master class in Las Vegas due to the miscarriage which almost ended her life. Koko mourned her loss for a few months, but that wasn't putting any money in her pockets. She got up, found a studio to rent, and went back to crafting edible treats to occupy her mind.

Cyrus wanted Koko to stay at home and try for another baby, but she was good on that. She realized her refusal to try for another baby may have been the reason Cyrus had gone elsewhere to procreate. With all the bullshit being placed before her, Koko no longer wanted a forever with him. Especially, knowing Cyrus had a son he was claiming in private only.

A woman could be everything to a man and he still wouldn't appreciate what was right in front of him. She refused to be one of the women who depended on him for what he could do for her. Koko was a go-getta and she would never allow a man to dictate what she could and couldn't have without his help. The bitches Cyrus frequented didn't have a pot to piss in, nor a window to throw it out of. That would never be the case with Kameeko Simmons.

After getting her mind together, Koko put her car in reverse and backed out of the parking space. Jackie emerged from the restaurant and she blew her horn before pulling off. It took twenty minutes for Koko to arrive at her studio in

Burnsville. She didn't live too far away so she wasn't worry about how long she would be there. Koko couldn't wait to jump into the sculpture she had drawn of a tiger and her cub. Being on the show gave Koko exposure she didn't think she would ever gain on her own recognition. Koko's Kakes & More was a hit with many people who carried a big name and she didn't short change herself either. The piece would make her bank account five thousand dollars heavier. She planned to give it her all too.

It was two in the afternoon and relief from the heat when Koko stepped foot into the place where nothing mattered except her mind working to perfect what she was doing. Shutting off her phone, she washed her hands and put on her apron as she prepared to work until the piece was finished. Once Koko had all the materials needed for her masterpiece, she got lost in what she loved with the first mold of chocolate she placed on the table. Minutes turned into hours in a blink of an eye.

"I thought you'd be here. Why haven't you answered your phone all day, Koko?"

Hearing Cyrus' voice put Koko into a mindset she really didn't want to be in. Trying her best to tune him out, she kept working on the hindlegs of her sculpture without even turning to address him. His face was the last thing she wanted to see and his lies were next in line.

"As you can see, I'm working. When I go missing, you know where I am, Cyrus. I can't say the same for you, though."

"What you mean by that?" he quizzed. "Go ahead and tell me what bullshit you done saw now. You've been acting funny since the day you didn't show up for my last visit."

"See, it's fucked up that you already know some shit done made its way back to me." Koko chuckled but never missed a beat with what she was doing. "Didn't I tell you I didn't give a fuck what you did in your spare time, long as the shit didn't make its way back to me?"

"Stop beating around the bush and tell me what's up." The quiver in Cyrus' voice told Koko he was nervous. As he should've been.

Throwing her tool onto the tabletop, Koko turned around abruptly and stood toe to toe with him. Cyrus had the audacity to stand there as if he hadn't been tucked away with a bitch who wanted the world, especially Koko to know she was sleeping with his slimy ass. Taking a step back, Cyrus waited for her to speak.

"One of your hoes thought it was important for me to know you were laid up in her dusty ass bed. Don't deny the shit because the bitch sent a pic to collaborate her story. If you're gonna cheat, please make sure the bitch is on a higher level than the woman you're already with. You out buying the low budget shit she can get on her own. With sheets up to her windows, that alone tells me you buying her ass the wrong shit."

"Who the fuck you talking about?"

Koko laughed because the nigga was acting as if he didn't know what the fuck she was talking about. Something clicked in her mind, causing her to laugh even harder. She was willing to play along, long as he wanted to play. "Well, damn, how many bitches you fuckin' that use sheets as curtains?"

"Cut the bullshit and tell me who sent some shit to you!" Cyrus had fire in his eyes because his hoes knew not to play with him when it came to Koko. She was off limits to anything he had going on outside of their relationship. He needed a name so he could check the bitch who thought going back to his woman was the thing to do. After he shook her ass around like a rag doll, he was going to cut her messy ass off.

"You're more worried about the who rather than the fact of me knowing you've been with a bitch." Koko smirked. "You know what? It doesn't even matter who sent the picture. You were in it. What I want to talk about is the son you produced. I'm not talking about the one who didn't make it into the world with me, either."

Cyrus stood silently as he took in the words Koko threw at him. In his mind he was trying to figure out how she knew about junior. Cyrus thought he covered his tracks well by moving Sheree far away from Koko. It hit him like a ton of bricks. Jackie had to be the one to disclose the information after promising to keep his secret under wraps.

"Don't even try to deny it because I already know the truth. The reason you didn't see me for our last visit is because I met Cyrus jr. and his mother in the waiting room. Hopefully, you were able to celebrate his first birthday. He deserves to have his father in his life. I won't make you choose between him and myself. I'm all for children growing up in two-parent homes."

Koko was livid and wasn't trying to hide anything she'd been keeping to herself. In her mind, she could strive further as a single woman instead of stressing over a man who didn't give a damn about her. Cyrus fucked up and it was time to lay it all on the table.

"Finding out you are a father is the straw that broke the camel's back. I've sat back being the best girlfriend ever while you fucked around with any and everything with a pussy." Koko turned her back to him and picked up the sharp tool to continue working. "I'm done, Cyrus. I'm tired of this back and forth shit we've been going through. It's obvious with me is not where you want to be."

"Ko, that's not my baby!" Cyrus yelled. "His mother named him after me in hopes that he is mine."

"Lower your voice. The little boy I saw is a spitting image of your ass. Down to your bowed legs. Go be a father because what we had is over. It was hard for me to hold my tongue all this time. You forced me to reveal what I know. My plans were to just walk away without incident. There's no way I can ever accept you having a child outside of me. I may love you, Cyrus, but I'll be damned if I sit back and act as if I'm the only woman in your life."

Cyrus stood in shock by Koko's choice of words. Never in a million years did he ever imagine Koko walking away from him. He tried his best to keep his infidelities from her, but Cyrus had done a shitty job keeping Cj a secret. Thinking back on his last visit day, Sheree and his son were there, but Koko wasn't. It never occurred to him they had crossed paths. Cyrus had to try his hand once again to get her to stay.

"I'll give you that. I know you just mad right now and I deserve everything you're doing. I love you, Koko. I'm scheduled for a DNA test on the baby next week. Don't give up on us."

"Are you really telling me not to give up when you're the one bringing all the bullshit? There isn't one instance when I've ever been accused of stepping out on you. I have always been all in from day one. I was committed to you and only you. You constantly went outside of what we had to do whatever your heart desired without wondering how it would make me feel. Maybe the man who's for me will be able to find me after I release the dead weight that's been holding me back, wasting my time for years. Now, you are free to do whatever the fuck you choose. I hope you find a woman who will be able to make you happy and open your eyes to love. In the meantime, get the fuck out of my studio."

Cyrus watched Koko chisel at the chocolate as if her life depended on it. Walking up to her, Cyrus placed his hand on the small of her back. Koko spun around like a ninja holding the sharp tool to his chin. The deadly stare she held, told Cyrus to leave her alone for a while. Without saying a word, Cyrus backed up and made his way to the door. Soon as he put his hand on the knob, Koko's voice stopped him in his tracks.

"Leave my key on the table. Please and thank you."

Doing as she asked, Cyrus took the key from his ring and left after placing it where she asked. He got into his whip and watched as Koko broke down where she stood. He felt like shit because he knew how much she loved him. Her heartache had nothing to do with him cheating. It was the fact that Cyrus gave another woman a child he only vowed to have with her. He didn't know how he would get back into her good graces, but Cyrus was not going to allow the love of his life to move on without him.

Chapter 2

Kameeko had Cyrus fucked up. Yeah, he was wrong for stepping out on her but she made it known she was too afraid to carry another baby and he wanted one of his own. Cyrus lowkey blamed Koko for the miscarriage because she kept stressing herself out about what he was doing when not with her. All she had to do was relax and concentrate on the accomplishments she had achieved. Cyrus felt he should've been the least of her worries after winning the top prize in front of millions on television.

It was a true fact Koko had gone through the entire process of being on the show alone because Cyrus was either hustling in the streets or cheating in peace. He cheered her on from Minnesota while she was in Vegas for months. Most of the time he was lying in bed watching Koko do her thang while being sucked off or rode into the sunset by Sheree. With his woman being hours away, Cyrus developed a relationship with a woman who understood him. So, he thought. Getting Sheree pregnant was never in the plans, but it happened.

When she delivered the news of carrying his baby, Cyrus wanted her to get an abortion. Sheree was already four months by the time she revealed the pregnancy along with an ultrasound photo. Seeing his child developing warmed his heart. Cyrus immediately moved Sheree to Maple Grove and into a home they could raise the baby together without word getting back to Koko. His plan only worked for so long because his woman of three years found out and was hurt in the worse way. Now, she didn't want anything to do with him.

After watching Koko cry her heart out for what seemed like forever, Cyrus drove away from the studio slowly with no destination in mind. He found his way to the house he purchased for Sheree and Cj, parking in the driveway behind her red 2023 Infinity QX55. He purchased the car for Sheree as a push gift right before she went into labor. Taking in the structure of the home, Cyrus shook his head. Koko didn't receive a fraction of what he'd given his baby mama and she had only been around a short time. That alone had him regretting what he'd done behind Koko's back.

The two women were like night and day, but both beautiful. Koko was the type of woman any man would want in his life. She had two degrees, her own business, and didn't want for nothing because she provided for herself. Koko was even there for Cyrus when he fell behind a few times. Sheree on the other hand barely graduated high school, was on government assistance, and relied on Cyrus for any and everything. The shit irked his nerve every time she came to him with her hand held out for money. Cyrus didn't mind providing for his son, but when it came to the way Sheree blew through funds, he was just not the nigga to give her the lifestyle she was seeking while sitting on her ass.

In the beginning, Cyrus splurged to get in good with her. Sheree had an expensive habit and he couldn't blame anyone but himself. At the rate she was going, Cyrus would be broke in a matter of years and he wasn't trying to go that route. After trying to get Koko to answer her phone several times, he finally sent her a text stating he still loved her. Getting out of his vehicle, Cyrus walked slowly up the stairs. The door opened before he made his way to the landing.

"Why didn't you call before showing up?" Sheree asked with her hand propped on her hip.

"Since when do I have to ask permission to come to *my* shit?" Cyrus shot back. "You seem to forget at times how the fuck you're able to even say this is yo' house. Without me, you would still be in North Minneapolis with the gutter rats. Stop playing with me, Ree." He entered the house, bumping her out of the way.

"What crawled up your ass and died?" Sheree asked slamming the door. "I haven't seen you in days, Cyrus. So, whoever pissed you off, take your frustrations out on them."

Ignoring what she had to say, Cyrus climbed the stairs to the bedroom. Sheree was on his ass talking crazy. He pulled his shirt over his head then threw it into the hamper before heading to the adjourning bathroom. Cyrus attempted to close the door but Sheree pushed it open with force. He was not in the mood to deal with her attitude after what he'd endured with Koko.

"Don't ever close a door in my face!"

"Gone with that bullshit, man," Cyrus said walking back into the bedroom emptying the contents from his pockets. After putting his phone on the dresser, Cyrus turned to Sheree. "Where's my son?"

"No, let's address your disrespectful actions first! What is your problem?"

"Sheree." Cyrus sighed as he pinched the bridge of his nose while shaking his head. "Where. Is. My. Son?"

The way his demeanor changed kind of spooked Sheree. She backed away from him a few feet because she didn't know how Cyrus would react when she told him Cj was at her mom's. Cyrus felt Sheree wasn't doing anything productive with her life so, his son should always be home with her. Plus, he didn't care for her people too much.

"He's at my mama's house. Now, back to you."

"At your mama's house? Why is my shorty not in this muthafucka with you? I've told you too many times I didn't want him over there!"

"They're his family, Cyrus. He is gonna spend time with them. Whenever my mama wants him, he's going. How 'bout that?" she sassed.

Cyrus chortled. "If that's the case, bitch, you need to be trying to find a fuckin' job to occupy your time. All that going out with ya friends, partying, drinking, and spending my money shit is over. I'm tired of stressing why you shouldn't keep taking him to her house. She didn't push him out; you did! Debbie shouldn't have him most of the damn week." Cyrus fumed.

"I don't even smoke and drink around CJ. I'm tired of my son being subjected to your brother's weed and yo' mama with them damn cancer sticks smoking around him. But it's me you call when he's having a fuckin' asthma attack! Go get my son!"

Cyrus was pissed because it was the same argument they had weekly. Sheree thought it wasn't a problem regardless of how much he stressed it was. Long as she was free of caring for their son, her ass was content with him not being around. Cyrus wasn't. He would rather Cj be with him than her relatives.

"I'm not going to get him because I already told my mama he could stay the night. I'm going out with my girls tonight."

Cyrus' lip curled into a snarl as he walked around the bed. Sheree followed his movements with her eyes. She could sense the anger he possessed without Cyrus even uttering a word. Once he started going through her purse, Sheree hurried across the room to stop him. There was no telling what he was going into her purse for.

"Get out of my purse, Cyrus!"

Shrugging her off, Cyrus kept searching. Sheree started hitting him in the back of his head with her fist. Cyrus refrained from reacting to the assault. Finally finding what he was looking for, he turned and was punched in his jaw. Basic instinct caused Cyrus to slap the shit out of her. Sheree palmed her cheek in shock.

"See. Keep yo' fuckin' hands to yo'self," he said putting the items from her purse in his pocket.

"Fuck the fact you put your hands on me. What did you take from my purse?" She snarled.

"*My* keys. You won't be playing chauffeur in the whip I paid for. Tell one of them bum bitches to come scoop you up. Oh, they can't. Get away from me, Sheree."

"That's my car!" she screamed, reaching for his pocket. "You bought it for me!"

"Now, I'm taking it back. The paperwork says Cyrus Davis the last time I checked. Meaning, it belongs to me. The only thing I asked you to do was bring my son home. You refused so…" he said walking away. "I'll pick him up when I get out the shower. Do whatever you gon' do for the night, but you won't be driving. I hope you have cash hidden somewhere because I took the card, too."

"I'm calling my brother to tell him you put your hands on me!"

Cyrus laughed. He wasn't worried about her brothers. Neither one of them were dumb enough to approach him about anything. They were both pussies anyway. "Tell them niggas. Am I supposed to be scared of two weak muthafuckas? Make sure you tell them why I slapped the taste out of yo' mouth while you at it. Fuck around and get they ass killed fuckin' with me."

Walking into the bathroom, Cyrus closed and locked the door behind him. His adrenaline was rushing, causing him to grip the counter to calm himself. The encounter wasn't the first between him and Sheree about their son, but it was the first time he put his hands on her. The shit made him feel some type of way because he didn't believe in a nigga hitting a woman in any shape, form or fashion. He'd seen men beat the fuck out of his mother growing up. The shit wasn't cool then, and it wasn't okay when he slapped Sheree.

Once she calmed down, he was going to apologize for his actions. After taking a few deep breaths, Cyrus turned the knobs to start the shower. He removed the rest of his clothes then stepped under the water to wash the day's events from his body. Koko was the image to invade his mind causing him to think hard about making things right with her.

While Cyrus was in the bathroom his phone vibrated on the dresser. Sheree sat on the side of the bed filling her best friend Freeda in on what transpired. She was in the middle of telling her about the altercation when her attention immediately went to the phone on the dresser as it vibrated again. Getting up, Sheree picked up the device and swiped up on the screen.

"Oh, bitch! His phone ain't locked," Sheree whispered. "Some bitch named Koko texted him."

"What is she talking about?" Freeda asked.

Sheree read the text and her heart started beating rapidly in her chest. She'd been with Cyrus for almost two years and the whole time he was in a relationship. Anger built within her in a matter of seconds. She wanted to go downstairs and microwave a bowl of water to throw on his cheating ass.

"Come on now! What the hell does the text say?" Freeda asked impatiently.

"I was reading the text and this nigga is the one who reached out to her first. The last text he sent said he still loved her. Her response was, *Love doesn't mean shit when you've lied to me for years. Cyrus, you have a fucking baby out there and I had to find out about it while you were locked up. Nothing can save the relationship we had. I meant what I said earlier. I'm done. Make the shit work with your baby mama. She can have your ass now.*"

"I told you his ass was too good to be true. I'm not going to say I told you so, but you were nothing but a sneaky link who ended up pregnant. What type of man hides a child he helped create? A muthafucka who had no intentions of being with you for the long haul. That's who."

"Freeda, stop rubbing the shit in my face. Cyrus played in my face and it explains why he came in with an attitude. The bitch cut him off and now he has his thumb up his ass about it."

The shower turned off and Sheree hurried to save Koko's number in her phone. She rushed to put Cyrus' phone back on the dresser after setting the message back to unread, then walked out of the room before he could exit the bathroom. Sheree went downstairs to the back patio to continue her conversation with Freeda. She wanted to tell her friend she would talk to her later but Freeda wasn't going away that easily.

"Okay, I'm outside. Finish saying what's on your mind because after tonight, I don't want to talk about this anymore."

"Sheree, don't tell me you're going to let this shit ride. You need to confront him about this shit. He was in a relationship with someone else while playing house with you and Cj! Outside of your circle, nobody knows this nigga has a kid! Y'all can coparent at this point because it's time for you to pack up and leave his ass alone."

"And go where, Freeda?" Sheree asked angrily. "There's no way I'm going back to sleeping in that twin size bed at my mama's house. I don't have a job and you know Debbie is only going to allow me to stay under her roof for a matter of time before she starts asking for money. Plus, Jojo lives there."

"You're making excuses. Cyrus laced your pockets for years. I know damn well you have some type of money put away for a rainy day."

Sheree hung her head low because she didn't have anything except the money Cyrus provided on the card for Cj. Every dime he'd given her throughout the years was spent immediately. Sheree always had to be on top of her game in order to showboat about the man she was dating. Saving money was her least worry because Cyrus had enough of it for the both of them. Whenever she asked for money, he pulled it from his pocket. Even when she didn't ask, he was dishing out funds but still, she didn't think about saving a penny. Long as she had Cj, Sheree knew his father would make sure he was taken care of.

"Your silence tells me you didn't. Am I correct?" Freeda asked softly.

"No, I haven't saved anything. I never thought I would have to worry about money while with Cyrus. There's plenty of money on the card he took from my purse."

"Why did he take the card?"

"He took my card and the keys to my car because I told him I wasn't going to pick up Cj from my mom's."

"Cyrus needs to get off his high horse. He's a fuckin' drug dealer and he don't want your son to spend time with his family. In my opinion, I believe he's just trying to stop you from going out to enjoy yourself. We both know nothing will happen to Cj while at Debbie's. That's a cop out to keep you isolated."

"He says there's too much smoking going on and Cj has asthma. I understand where he's coming from and I'm going to talk to mama about it. But I don't think stopping him from spending time with his grandma is going to solve anything. It's not like she can come here to visit."

Tears welled in Sheree's eyes. The thought of Cyrus cutting her off was making her emotional. A plan was formulating in her mind as she sat quietly. Sheree didn't have any choice except to get a job. She was willing to do whatever it took to get back into Cyrus' good graces. She wasn't going to even mention what she read in his phone. It would only cause more friction between them and she didn't want any tension in the house when her son was present.

"See what I mean? He doesn't even want your family to come to the house. And what the hell taking the card is going to do? You still need it to take care of my godson."

"I'm sure he's going to give it back so I can do that. Cyrus just doesn't want me to go out to the club spending the money on myself."

"Yeah, okay. Well, I think after all this shit, you need to come out with us. I have a rental for the weekend so coming to get you won't be a problem. What do you say?" Freeda asked.

The sliding door opened and Cyrus appeared dressed in a pair of joggers, a t-shirt, and a pair of Jordans. Sheree told Freeda to hold on and muted the phone. She sat quietly waiting for Cyrus to say whatever was on his mind.

"I want to apologize for slapping you. I'm not the type of nigga to beat on women. When you punched me in the jaw, my reflexes reacted. It shouldn't have happened and I'm sorry. We will have to talk about your future plans."

"What do you mean my future plans? Are you putting me out of the house?" Sheree asked astonished.

"No, I'm not putting you out. Why would I do that when you have my son? You're jumping the gun, Sheree. I think you should think about finding a job. On some real shit. All you do is spend money without bringing anything in. It's not that I don't want to provide for you. I've been doing it from day one. Now, I want you to establish something for yourself. Hell, you can go back to school. Long as you're doing something constructive. The last thing I want you to do is depend on me all the time."

Nodding in agreement, Sheree bit her bottom lip to prevent herself from cursing him out. Instead, she told him what he wanted to hear. "I'm going to put in applications on Monday. Tonight showed me things between us can change in the blink of an eye. I should be able to provide for Cj without your help."

"Sheree, you will never have to take care of our son alone. I will always be there when he needs me." he said honestly. "Call yo' mama and tell her to have Cj ready. I'm about to go get him. If you're not here when I get back, have fun tonight." Cyrus turned to walk away then doubled back. "Don't set your brothers up for failure. I just want my son. Nothing more, mothing less."

24

Cyrus left leaving Sheree sitting outside thinking about what he'd said. Her phone rang in her hand and it was Freeda calling back. She let the phone go to voicemail but it didn't stop her friend from calling again.

"I'm good, Free. Cyrus came in to talk. Sorry about that. He's going to get Cj."

"Call Jojo and Steve. They need to know that nigga out here playing the role of Ike Turner!"

"I'm not calling them because it's not even worth the drama. I punched him first so, I'm at fault."

"You better than me because his ass would be whooped! Anyway, am I coming to pick you up or what?" she asked.

"Yeah. I'm about to go get ready now. As a matter of fact, come get me now. I'll get ready at your house. I don't want to be here when Cyrus returns."

"That's what the fuck I'm talkin' about! We gon' find you another muthafucka to lay under. Fuck Cyrus. He's not the only nigga with money out in these streets. I'm on my way and make sure you are overly cute too."

Freeda didn't like Cyrus the first night Sheree met him. They were in the club and women were in his face from the time he walked in the door. Sheree made it a point to stay in close proximities of Cyrus until she gained his attention. Her intentions when she and her friends decided to go out was to snag a man with money.

Sheree was a twenty-four old who still lived with her mother. She was a manager at Arby's making sixteen dollars an hour. Working fifty plus hours a week, Sheree earned twelve hundred dollars every pay period before taxes. She was over the long days with mediocre pay. At the time she needed a man financially and Cyrus just so happened to be her way out. It took a couple months of playing a role but her performance paid off in the end.

The night Sheree decided to have sex with Cyrus scaled the deal. She pulled out all the tricks from her hoe bag and put on a magic show where it counted. Sheree didn't hold back. Never being the one to go all out sexually, she sucked toes, dick, balls, and allowed Cyrus to have his way with her however he pleased. Sheree allowed him to fuck her in every hole in her body until his nuts were drier than the Sahara Desert. Then the money started flowing to her liking.

Freeda hung up after Sheree agreed to be ready when she arrived. Locking up, she walked up the stairs to her room to pack a bag. The thought of working was heavily on Sheree's mind. She knew her work experience would never earn her the amount of money Cyrus gave her on a weekly basis. Her time would be limited the moment she had to punch a clock for the white man.

**

Sitting in the driver's seat of his car, Cyrus unlocked his phone to text Koko when he noticed she had already reached out to him. He smiled as he opened the message but it was short-lived. The words Koko said hurt his heart. Cyrus realized he had fucked up. Koko washed her hands of him and there was no coming back from it. He put the car in drive and made his way to Debbie's house to get his son.

Cyrus drove in silence until he couldn't take it anymore. Hitting the Apple Music app on his phone, he connected the device to the Bluetooth. He decided to check out the Mo3 *Legend* album which had been released the day before. The track *Came up* guided him to his destination. Mo3 was a very talented artist and Cyrus was saddened when the news about his death was announced. Cyrus could relate to the music because he lived the life of the streets. The song took him back to when he was trying to come up in the game.

He started out in the game with the help of his uncle Silas. He was sixteen when he was put in position to deliver a package. Being a young jit, the dealer Cyrus delivered to strong armed him and took his product. Knowing he couldn't go back to his uncle without the money, Cyrus had to make a decision. He was scared shitless because he knew Silas didn't play about his money. Family or not, there would've been repercussions if he showed up empty handed. Walking around the corner, Cyrus waited until the men surrounding the dealer left and he made his move.

With the pocketknife Silas gifted him for his birthday, Cyrus crept along the side of the car and plunged the blade in the neck of the dealer. He then took the bag with the product from the passenger seat and another that was on the floor in the back. Cyrus ran clumsily back to his uncle's house. After telling Silas what happened, Cyrus was rewarded with ten thousand dollars. That was a lot of money for a sixteen-year-old.

Word got out about the kid who killed a well-known drug dealer the next day and there was a bounty put on Cyrus' head. Silas thought it would be best for Cyrus to move out of Alabama and head to Minnesota to live with his grandma. They hit the road later that night. Silas made sure Cyrus was taken care of. He pulled up on his nephew weekly then eased in with dope on the sly when Cyrus turned seventeen. They had to keep things under the radar because Cyrus' granny didn't approve of what Silas did to make money. She never wanted that lifestyle for her grandson.

Cyrus was hesitant to go full throttle into the game…until his mama was killed. When Silas suggested he moved from Alabama, Cyrus didn't want to leave his mother. He was an only child and he was all she had. The man his mother was with at the time was very abusive. Cyrus would walk in from school to his mother being beaten like a man. His presences always stopped the assault so, he made it his business to be around so she wouldn't have to go through the abuse. He pled with her to put the nigga out but she always told Cyrus to mind his business. His mama was the reason he really didn't want to move but he didn't have a choice.

Cyrus was lying in his room listening to music when Silas entered with a somber expression on his face. Right away he knew something was wrong. Sitting on the bed, Silas ran his hand down his face then looked at him.

"Cyrus, something happened back in Alabama. Landa died today."

The words, "Landa died," echoed in his ears. The rage overpowered the hurt Cyrus was feeling in that moment. His heart hollowed out at the thought of never hearing the voice of the woman he loved with everything in him. Tears rolled down his face but he didn't feel the wetness. All he could think about was the screams of his mother being beaten before his eyes. The fact of not being there to save her one last time, activated something inside of him.

"What happened?" Cyrus croaked out. he wanted to know what caused his mother's demise.

"Jerome beat and shot her. His ass is on the run but I'm going to find him," Silas promised. "He's not going to leave Mobile."

"I know he won't because I'm going to make sure of it."

"Cyrus, I want you to sit back—"

"And do what, let you handle it? Nah, it ain't gon' happen. I told that nigga to keep his hands to himself on many occasions. I'm not the same lil nigga who had to put on a brave face to say something. I'm now a monster who has the intentions of tearing his muthafuckin' head off. He killed my mama!"

The memory was a hard one for Cyrus to reflect on. He tried his best not to go back to the day he had to close the casket on his favorite girl. The image that did make its way back was when he found Jerome and made his ass eat dirt. It took a year to catch up with him, but vengeance didn't have an expiration date. Jerome didn't have a chance to say anything before a bullet was lodged into his left eye. Cyrus laid him down then caught a flight back to Minnesota. Life for him had been up from there.

They ask me how I came up
'Cause I stayed down

Why would I change up? Them people know my name
It's crazy how I got the fame
My life so dangerous
Ima always stay the same
Even when they change it up

Cyrus cruised on the highway while checking out the rest of the album and he liked it actually. When he was closer to Debbie's house, the environment changed drastically from the neighborhood he'd just left. There was a reason he moved his son away from Sheree's family. He refused to subject him to the life of inner city living. Yeah, there weren't many black folks that way, but Cj would be able to go outside and play without worrying about getting shot. Another reason was to keep the shit he was doing away from his son as well. Cj was never going to experience selling drugs because Cyrus was going to make sure he did more in life.

As he parked in front of the apartment complex, Cyrus got out of the car and walked to the front door. He pushed the button to buzz inside Debbie's place. No one answered. Repeating the gesture, Cyrus waited patiently for someone to open the door. Glancing at his watch, he became overly irritated because he figured Sheree's mama was purposely not answering. Cyrus adjusted his Glock on his hip out of habit even though he had a feeling he was going to make that muthafucka sing. Instead of ringing the bell again, Cyrus snatched his phone from his pocket and called Sheree.

"Yes, Cyrus," she said soon as the phone connected.

"I'm at yo' mama's and she not answering the door. Call her ass right now and find out where she is."

"I was about to call you but you beat me to it. She's at my aunt Daphne's house."

"Aight," he said ending the call.

Cyrus headed to his car with steam resonating from his pores. He knew there was about to be some shit soon as he pulled up. Debbie only visited her sister when they were on bullshit. Daphne had two sons who were jealous as fuck of Cyrus. They grilled him whenever he decided to accompany Sheree to a family gathering. He understood though. Both Jerrod and Jermaine were bums who wanted to be on Cyrus' team. He refused to put them on because they were irresponsible and couldn't be trusted. Cyrus knew they would bump heads at every turn when the time came for them to take orders from the man, they called *the lil nigga.* So, they held animosity against him as if it meant something.

It took Cyrus ten minutes to arrive at Daphne's house. Just as he thought, Sheree's brothers and her cousins were sitting on the porch smoking. The moment Cyrus parked his jet black metallic 1970 Chevrolet Chevelle SS, one would've thought there was a decayed body nearby the way those niggas noses were turned up. The hate was at an all-time high and the shit made Cyrus grin from ear-to-ear. They rose to their feet when the driver's door opened, all four of them descended the stairs. Cyrus laughed as he walked toward the house without fear.

"Aye, Cyrus," Sheree's brother Jojo called out hiking up his pants. "What's this I hear about you putting yo' hands on my sister?"

"Man, go get my son. I didn't come here for this bullshit," Cyrus snapped. "You muthafuckas on this thug shit and that's why ya pockets flat. Worrying about the wrong shit."

"You didn't answer the question, nigga!" Jerrod snarled.

"I'm not obligated to either. The fuck. I hope Sheree told the whole truth of the matter," Cyrus said taking a step forward.

"Sheree ain't said shit! But I bet Freeda didn't lie about what was told to her. So, nigga, that tells me you did hit my muthafuckin' cousin," Jermaine barked, folding his arms over his chest.

Cyrus chuckled as he shook his head. "Equal rights, equal lefts. That's neither here nor there I see. Y'all on good bullshit and got something to get off y'all chests. So, let's get down to business. Tell Sheree to keep her hands to herself and I'll do the same."

"Hand over the keys to her car and I'll think about letting you leave without fuckin' you up." Jojo had the nerve to give an ultimatum and Cyrus wasn't with it.

"Come get 'em yourself."

Soon as Cyrus said the last statement, Jermaine lunged at him swinging spot on but Cyrus dodged the blow hitting him with three quick punches. Stumbling back stunned; Jermaine wasn't expecting the power behind the punch because Cyrus was small compared to him. Cyrus was five feet ten inches with a muscular upper build. Jermaine on the other hand was six feet four with a lean build and slow with his movements. He was no match for the boxing experience Cyrus held under his belt.

Before Jermaine could redeem himself, Cyrus hit him again in the left temple dropping his big ass. His brother Jerrod ran up catching Cyrus off guard and got a couple punches in of his own. Cyrus shook the hits off then grabbed him by the throat slamming Jerrod onto his back. Steve pulled a tool from his hip pointing it at Cyrus' head. The gun didn't put any fear in the man standing before him. In fact, Steve's actions made Cyrus madder than he already was.

"You ain't so tough now, huh, nigga?" Jojo laughed.

"I'm forever tough, muthafucka! The question is, are you?" Cyrus smirked. "You pulled that shit, now use it if you got the heart."

At that moment the door open and Debbie came out with Cj cradled in her arms. She was smiling until realization of what was taking place clicked in her mind. Cj struggled to get out of her arms but Debbie was obviously afraid shots would be fired.

"Daddy!"

Jojo's head turned swiftly at the sound of his nephew's voice but Steve's eyes remained trained on Cyrus. There was no doubt he wanted to pull the trigger. Steve knew he

31

couldn't go through with it in the presence of his nephew. The resentment would've been crucial between them further in life.

"Yo' ass been saved by the muthafuckin' bell. Keep yo' hands off my sister! You ain't her damn daddy, nigga."

"I'm her daddy every time my dick caresses her folds," Cyrus smirked. "You fucked up not taking that shot though."

Cyrus walked away as Steve tucked his Glock. He had no worries turning his back on the pussy ass niggas because they weren't about that life. Cyrus was and he had every intention of finishing what they started. Just not in front of his son. Jerrod and Jermaine stood to the side waiting for Cyrus to bleed on the pavement. They were bent out of shape because the nigga was still standing. Prying Cj from his grandma then made his way to his whip. As he strapped his son into the car seat, Jojo's voice stopped his movements.

"This ain't over. You better watch yo' fuckin' back."

"Don't throw idle threats, brah. It's not good for your health. Plus, you know where I be. Pull up when you ready."

Cyrus knew they weren't on shit. He rounded the front of the car, got inside and started the engine. Cyrus glance over at Sheree's people one more time before nodding and driving off.

"Daddy, gun. I want gun," Cj said happily clapping his hands.

"No! I'll buy you some cars. You not getting a gun ever!"

Hearing his son ask for a gun pissed Cyrus off to the max. for his one-year-old to even be able to say the word told him his punk ass uncles taught him that shit. He was going to raise his son to be a better man than he was and Cyrus was going to fight until he took his last breath to make sure Cj didn't get sucked into the street life.

Not wanting to go back to Sheree's, Cyrus decided to head to his apartment. As he drove in silence Cyrus found himself in front of Koko's place. Exiting the vehicle Cyrus rounded the car to get his son out of the back seat. He made his way to the front door and pushed the button beside Koko's name on the panel. It had been a while since he had to stand in wait for her to buzz him in. Cyrus hated the fact of Koko forcing him to give the keys to her apartment back.

"Who is it?" Koko's angelic voice flowed throw the intercom.

"It's me, babe." Koko didn't say anything after Cyrus identified himself. "Koko, it's me," he said again.

He was about to ring the bell again when the door was snatched opened. An upset Koko appeared then her demeanor turned into anger in a flash. The way her nose flared, anybody else would've left the premises. Not Cyrus. He stood his ground.

"You must've fell and hit your head."

"What you talkin' about? I came over so we could discuss us and you come down mad."

"Are you serious right now?" She snapped. "There's nothing to talk about, especially when you showed up with the very thing that ended our relationship."

"Thing? My son is a product of me, and far from a thing. Check yo' mouth, Koko. He is innocent in all this shit."

"You know what? You are absolutely correct. He is innocent, but his dumb ass daddy isn't. So, why would you bring him here?"

"If we're going to work on our relationship—"

"Who told you we were working on anything?" Koko asked cutting Cyrus off. "It sure wasn't me. Last I checked, you were informed the relationship was over. Meaning, I don't want shit else to do with you. Bringing that baby here didn't help your chances at all. Not that you had a slim chance anyway. I'm going to say this in a way you should understand this time. Go back to your baby mama and stay the fuck away from me!"

"Koko—" Was all Cyrus could get out before the door was closed in his face. He stood in the same spot for Lord knows how long until Cj brought him back to reality by tapping him on the chest. Cyrus looked down at a young version of himself and forced a smile.

"Eat, eat, daddy."

"I got you, lil homie. Let's go home."

"Mommy."

As much as Cyrus wanted to go to his own spot, he buckled his son back in the car seat and headed back to Sheree's. Koko's rejection kept him company the entire way. Cyrus shook his head because he fucked up a good thing for a massive amount of drama. Sheree opened a can of worms when she ran her mouth to Freeda. The blood of her family was going to be on her hands whenever them niggas came for him.

Chapter 3

Cyrus had the nerve to pop up at Koko's doorstep with his son in hand. She kept the hurt at bay and it was a hard task to achieve. The moment she entered her apartment the tears cascaded down her face. Seeing the two of them together took Koko back in time to the day she lost the baby she carried for four months. With everything that had taken place, she dodged a bullet. It was never in Koko's plans to raise a baby alone. She always envisioned life as a mother with a husband by her side. Living in an apartment wasn't part of the equation either and Cyrus proved he was not husband material for any woman.

Wiping the tears away quickly, Koko had too much to be happy about to even allow Cyrus to get her down. She had just arrived home from her studio. While there she received a call from a locomotive company who wanted her to make a piece of the new train they would be presenting at their event. The event was a month out and Koko accepted right away after being told she was recommended by one of her elite clients. Even though she still had at least two or three days to finish the tigers she was working on, Koko couldn't pass up the opportunity. The owner emailed the information and also an invitation to the event for her to attend.

The ringing of her phone brought Koko out of her thoughts. She rushed to her purse for the device and looked at the screen before answering. Seeing Jackie's name made her let out the breath she was holding in after praying it wasn't Cyrus.

"What's up, Jackie?"

"Are you home," she asked.

"Yeah, I just got in. Why?"

"My latest boo thang is having a party at Reign. Do you wanna go with me?"

Koko really wasn't feeling Jackie at the moment because in the pit of her soul she had an inkling Jackie knew about Cyrus' secrets. Koko wasn't going to address her thoughts with her friend just yet. Time would reveal what she already thought in due time. She had never been to the club and was always down for a new experience. That night she was going to go out, enjoy herself and celebrate the successes coming her way.

"I'll go. Getting out can do me some good right about now."

"Cool, I'll come pick you up."

"No need. I'm going to drive. You know when I'm ready to go, you not. So…"

"You on bullshit, Ko. Please don't leave after an hour of us getting there." Silence overtook the line then Jackie huffed loudly. "If you don't want to go, say that."

"Didn't I say I would go? Stop with the guilt tripping. Now, can I get ready?"

"Okay. I'll see you soon." Jackie said ending the call.

Jackie had every right to be worried about Koko leaving the club. The atmosphere would determine if she stay or leave. The folks in Minnesota were no better than the riff raff in Chicago so anything could pop off in a drop of an eye. Koko always studied her surroundings. When the vibe wasn't right, she was ready to go where she paid bills.

Walking to the back of her apartment, Koko entered her bedroom. She sat on the side of the bed in silence. After years of dealing with Cyrus' disrespect, Koko had truly made up her mind. She had enough and there was no going back.

There was no amount of begging, pleading, nor apologies that would remotely force her to forgive him. Love wasn't enough when it came to Cyrus. She believed he loved her but the more she thought about it, Cyrus loved the thought of having Koko in his life. The level of love was top tier...coming from Koko alone. At that point, Koko decided the love she was capable of giving would be put into herself from here on out. She made a vow to never pour more into another than she poured into herself.

"The next man will have to come correct or not at all. As a matter of fact, that's my damn problem. I've been giving boys my attention."

Koko vented to herself coming to a conclusion as of why she was going through her ordeal. Her status as an entrepreneur heightened in the past year. Koko was in a league of her own. She could've leveled up from the start but for one, she didn't want to buy property in Minnesota. After years of living in the state, Koko never felt at home from the moment she arrived. Two, she never wanted to flaunt her success in front of Cyrus. Koko always allowed him to be the man in the relationship and provide. Even though the only thing he provided was apology gifts when he got caught messing up. That alone was the reason Koko never fully revealed her true finances with him.

Taking a deep breath, Koko stood then walked to her closet to find an outfit to wear for the night. As she sifted through the items a thought entered her mind. Would Cyrus be at the party? In all hindsight she hoped not because the hour Jackie thought she'd spend at the club would definitely be cut to minutes the moment she laid eyes on her ex for sure.

Koko decided on a leather halter top with matching shorts. Being on the short side, she opted for a pair of six-inch Red Bottom stilettos. Laying her clothes out on the bed, Koko wrapped her hair then headed for the shower. She plugged in the flat iron so it would be nice and hot when she was ready to attack her hair. Koko placed a shower cap over her head then stepped into the shower to take care of her hygiene.

After cleansing herself thoroughly, Koko moisturized her body then got dressed. She straightened her long tresses before applying a light layer of makeup to her face. Admiring herself in the mirror, Koko blew a kiss to herself. She'd come a long way from the little girl who was called ugly by the woman who had given her life. Nadine Simmons was light skinned and beautiful on the outside. It was the inside that was rotten to the core and ugly. The words rang in her ears as if her mother was standing beside her in the room.

You're black and ugly just like your no-good ass daddy. No man is going to want a dark-skinned woman, so I hope you're ready to use what you got to get what you want. You will never have kids because no one is going to procreate with you. You're not going to be shit but a cum bucket. In other words, you will grow to be the perfect hoe.

Tears ran down Koko's face, smearing her makeup. The hurtful words always came out of the blue when Koko praised herself. She had skin the color of milk chocolate and Koko said affirmations to uplift herself when her mother wouldn't. It took a very long time to get to the confident place she was in about her complexion. There was no way she was going to backslide that night.

Instead of sitting wallowing in the past, Koko thought about all she'd accomplished without the help of her mother and a wide smile replaced the frown. The money she had in the bank…hers. Her car…hers. The success…she did that. As Koko thought about all she had endured alone, her chest swelled.

Her mother did the bare minimum for Koko when she was growing up. Her sisters and brother were treated so much better because they looked more like their mother. Koko was considered the black sheep even though she had the best grades, went to college and obtained degrees in business. Her siblings not so much.

Koko's sister Daniyah was two years younger and she had three kids, on government assistance, and dropped out of high school her sophomore year. Dee was the type who went after a man who would give her any and everything she needed. That only got her so far because it only lasted so long because of her attitude. She didn't have sense to save or invest the money to accumulate more funds for herself. Since Koko had splurged on her last baby and even bought for the other two, Dee thought it was okay to call her sister every time one of the kids needed something.

Ariel was the next sibling in line at twenty-three. She followed Koko's footsteps and actually attended college. She didn't graduate because while in college, Ariel ventured off into the life of fast money. Her mindset was, why did she need to continue her education when she could go dance for a couple hours and make thousands of dollars. Ariel lived in Atlanta and started dancing at *Magic City.* She made good money and Koko was happy for her. Long as it kept her sister out of her pockets.

Donald, her only brother, was the baby of the family. He was spoiled and entitled; so he thought. Koko's mother babied him to the point of when he graduated high school, he had no intentions of ever obtaining a job. Why should he have to work when Nadine provided any and everything for him. At twenty-one, Don was a father to a two-year old daughter named Diamond. And of course, his mother was the sole provider for her as well. When her phone rang with her brother's name on the display, Koko automatically answered with *I'm not sending any money.*

To her family, excluding Ariel, Koko was the cash cow. She was so accustomed to saying no that sometimes she didn't answer at all. The disrespect from her mother was the reason she packed up and moved without their knowledge. No one had called to see if she was alive and breathing for two years. The moment Koko made her appearance on television, then everyone was proud. When she won the top prize, her phone was ringing off the hook on a daily basis. The birth of Koko's Kakes & More put the icing on the cake. Nadine figured Koko's money was automatically hers and that just wasn't the case. She didn't owe her mother a damn thing and Koko would forever stand on never doing anything for her.

Reapplying her makeup, Koko grabbed her small Michael Kors purse and put her phone, ID, and her lip gloss inside. With her keys in hand, she turned the lights off and headed for the door. Locking up her apartment, Koko walked slowly down the stairs. As she opened the door to step outside, she spotted Jackie's car next to her own. She wondered what her friend was doing there when they had agreed to meet at the club.

"Is something wrong?" Koko asked as she stopped at Jackie's window.

"No, I just wanted to make sure we show up at the club together."

Koko didn't believe her at all so, she voiced it. "Jackie, you are lying. You didn't trust that I was coming."

"You got me."

Rolling her eyes, Koko stuck up her middle finger and pushed the button on her key fob to unlock the door to her vehicle. Automatically turning the air on, Koko was ready to see what the night had to offer. She connected her phone to the Car play and *Hiss* by Megan Thee Stallion blared through the speakers.

I just wanna kick this shit off by sayin' fuck y'all

I ain't gotta clear my name on a muthafuckin' thang

Every time I get mentioned, one of you bitch ass niggas get twenty-four hours of attention

I'm finna get this shit off my chest and lay it to rest. Let's go

Jackie backed out of the space with Koko right behind her. She jammed to the song reciting the lyrics as they hopped on the highway. It took them fifteen minutes to arrive at their destination and the crowd was thick. Jackie pulled up to valet and both of them handed their vehicles over to be parked. Koko stood to the side as her friend made her way over.

"Girl, I just found out Nelly is going to be in the building tonight! I forgot he was going to be in town for the *Together Again Tour* with Janet Jackson. He's having his after party here!"

Koko would've loved to see both Janet Jackson and Nelly in concert but work kept her out of the loop of what was happening in the entertainment world. It was great she may get a glimpse of Nelly at the least. The line into the building was long as hell. Koko didn't think there would be any way they would even be able to get inside. Walking in the direction of the line, Jackie's voice stopped her in her tracks.

"Where are you going?" she called out.

"To the back of the line."

"Nah, we not doing that tonight. Follow me."

Jackie led them to the front of the line and right up to the first available bouncer. The way he looked at them told Koko he was about to give them hell and refuse to let them inside. Without acknowledging Jackie, the man motioned for the next person to step forward and that pissed her off.

"Do you not see us standing here?" She asked nice as she could.

"The line is back there." He pointed. "Either go wait in line like everyone else, or go yo' ass home."

"I'm not doing neither of the two. Watch me work."

Jackie took out her phone and tapped away on the screen. She looked up with a smirk and stepped back watching the door. The bouncer allowed about ten people in the building before the door opened and a big nigga stepped out looking

41

around. Jackie moved in his direction and the bouncer grabbed her by the arm. What did he do that for?"

"Do we have a muthafuckin' problem?" the mystery man asked.

The bouncer looked over his shoulder and his eyes bulged. "Lowkey, what you mean, my guy?"

"You got yo' hand on something that belongs to me. I don't know why I had to come out here when all you had to do was let her in when she mentioned my name."

"Sh-She didn't mention your name."

"That's because you were rude from jump and didn't give me the opportunity to mention anything before you dismissed me," Jackie spat.

The bouncer had nothing to say in return. Instead, he just waited for what Lowkey had for him. When Lowkey grabbed Jackie by the hand, he kissed her on the lips then turned back to the bouncer.

"Next time don't be so quick to react. There's a reason you have a list of names in yo' pocket. Use that muthafucka. Next time I won't be so nice. As a matter of fact, when you see this woman, let her in. No questions asked unless I tell you otherwise."

With that, Lowkey and Jackie walked off, leaving Koko and the bouncer behind. When Jackie realized Koko wasn't by her side, she turned and waved her along. Koko had never seen Lowkey before and wondered where he'd come from and how long Jackie had been involved with him. By the way he bossed up on the bouncer, Lowkey held some type of weight around there. Walking behind them Koko took in the environment of the club. She had to admit, it was nice.

The music was loud and the patrons in the club were diverse. Lowkey had a section in the back of the club. When Koko entered, she wanted to turn around immediately. There were a few of Cyrus' homies in attendance. She didn't want to party with anyone associated with her ex because all of them knew what Cyrus did outside of her. Koko mood went from excitement to not wanting to be in the building at that point. Jackie noticed the change in her friend and came over immediately.

"What's wrong?" she whispered in Koko's ear.

"Is Cyrus coming this party, Jackie? I don't want to be here with him. Cyrus and I broke up today and I want to keep it that way without incident."

Jackie had a shocked expression but she had to put on a show so Koko wouldn't suspect her knowing the details already. Cyrus called her soon as he left Koko's apartment and suggested Jackie to get her out of the house. He didn't want her to sit home crying about what he had done to her. Jackie didn't want to be in the middle of what was going on between her two best friends, but she was stuck. The hard part was keeping the secret from Koko because if she found out Jackie knew everything, their friendship would be over.

"No. He didn't say anything about coming."

"If he shows up, I'm leaving," Koko said.

Nodding in understanding, Jackie took Koko's hand, leading her to an empty seat. There was more alcohol on the tables than behind the bar. Tequila always put Koko at ease, so Jackie poured her a double shot and handed it to her. Downing the drink, Koko swayed to the music as she sat observing everyone around her. The DJ was playing Latin tunes and the dance floor was full. No matter the ethnicity of the people dancing, a time was being had without any drama. It was the type of party Koko liked and could enjoy.

Being comfortable in the establishment, Koko decided to loosen up and have fun. She poured herself another drink with a splash of pineapple juice. As she put the straw up to her mouth, Austin, one of Cyrus workers approached her with a sly smile. Koko didn't like him because whenever Cyrus' back was turned or he wasn't around, Austin always tried to shoot his shot. He should've known Koko was not the type to fuck around with anyone associated with her man. She didn't know what kind of deal their crew had going on, she wasn't trying to partake in the bullshit. Koko also never told Cyrus about what Austin did because she didn't want his death on her conscious.

"Kameeko, I'm surprised to see you here." Austin looked around as if he was searching for someone. He turned back around licking his lips with pure lust in his eyes. "Where's Cyrus?" he asked.

"I don't know." Koko replied nonchalantly.

"That's ya man. You should always know where he is and what he's doing."

Koko had a bad feeling about Austin, but she also knew if she gave him enough bait, he would reveal what she perceived already. Pretending to ponder on his statement, Koko took a sip of her drink. "Nope. Cyrus is no longer my concern. Now if you would excuse me, I'm trying to have a good time. Not hold a conversation about my past."

"So, you finally realized Cyrus wasn't the man for you, huh?" Austin cracked.

Koko looked at him crazy as he sat down beside her. Austin was trying to get cozy after hearing she and Cyrus was no longer together. Austin thought he had a chance to weasel his way into Koko's life, but it would be a waste of his time. He knew Cyrus was no good for Koko and didn't deserve her. So, he was going to make sure she would never go back to the nigga. When Koko didn't respond to him, Austin went in for the kill.

"You do know Cyrus was cheating on you the entire time y'all was together, right? He had so many bitches coming through the block then come home to you. I'm glad you ended that shit and found your worth. Cyrus ain't shit and will never be shit. On top of that, he got a whole child out here. Did you know?"

Taking a sip of her drink, Koko chuckled as she listened to Austin turn into a whole fuck nigga right before her eyes. She didn't know the dynamics of Cyrus' infidelities, but his boy was about to fill her in on everything Koko didn't have a clue about.

Austin cocked his eyebrow at her actions and cleared his throat as he adjusted himself in his seat. "I'm not trying to hurt you more than he already has. What I have told you probably came as a shock. Somebody had to tell you though."

Koko finished off her drink and put the glass on the table. She turned toward Austin crossing her legs. He smiled as if he she was giving him her undivided attention. The music kept everybody entertained including Jackie. Koko looked across the section and her friend was all about Lowkey. She wasn't mad because Austin was giving her an earful, but it was time to return the favor.

"Austin, let me enlighten you on a few things," she said leaning in closer so he could hear her clearly. "Cyrus *has* cheated more times than I would like to count. How long he's been doing it is not my concern. The problem I have with what you disclosed is why did you choose now to tell me? See, you have come to my home and been in my presence for years and not once have you attempted to put a buzz in my ear."

"It wasn't—"

"Hold on, I'm not finished," Koko said holding her hand up to stop him from talking. "Far as the baby situation, I just found out about Cj, but you knew about him from the start. Fuck you and Cyrus! You could've kept that shit to yourself. You were quick to reveal things after the fact and I can't ride with that. So, whatever you thought you were going to accomplish tonight, just know you failed." Koko got up and walked away from him.

At that moment, Nelly entered the building and that's when the real party started. Jackie joined her in the front of the venue and they danced the night away as Nelly entertained the crowd with his classic hits. It was an entire concert in the building and Koko loved every bit of it. Nelly exited the stage after about an hour and the party didn't stop.

"I'll be back. I have to go to the bathroom," Jackie said walking away.

Staring after her friend, Koko was baffled that she wasn't asked if she had to relieve her bladder. She made her way through the crowd making her way to the restroom. As Koko pushed the door open a little bit, Jackie's voice paused her entry. There was anger in her friend's tone and that alone put Koko on alert in case she needed to beat somebody's ass.

"I saw you dancing on that nigga and kissing him in the mouth, Sheree! What type of shit are you on?" Jackie snapped. "What if Cyrus had walked in this bitch?"

"He ain't coming nowhere. His ass is at home with his son. Get away from me with that bullshit. You always eye spying for your best friend even though you know he ain't shit."

"What are you talking about?"

Koko stood outside the door in pure shock of what she was hearing. What happens in the dark always comes to light and Jackie proved that shit. She also showed Koko where her loyalty truly lied and it was obviously with Cyrus. She knew the nigga's baby mama on a first name basis and it was a telling sign of Jackie knowing her on a personal level. The way Koko's blood boiled had her inner self fighting not to go in there and beat the hell out her *friend*. With friends like that, who needed enemies?

"Jackie, don't play dumb with me. You and Cyrus are close, so you know about the female named Koko. Now how long has she and Cyrus been together?"

Jackie's response was going to determine how Koko would move next. In her mind, Jackie better choose wisely because her fighting skills were depending on her. Biting down on her bottom lip, Koko waited for the moment she would step into the bathroom and wreak havoc.

"Koko is his ex. Cyrus don't want anything to do with her. Why are you worried about the next bitch anyway? You have the kid, the house, the car, and the money that comes along with the man himself. All that other shit is irrelevant." Jackie paused. "Koko lives in an apartment, and no Cyrus don't help her with bills, nor does she have a no-balance card either."

Koko had enough. She couldn't stand there listening to her so call friend talk down on her as if she wasn't shit. Kicking off her shoes once the door closed behind her, Koko didn't give a damn about what could've been on the bottom of her feet from the floor. There was one thing on her mind and that was beating the snot out of Jackie's phony ass.

"Since you're in here telling my business, don't leave out the reason Cyrus doesn't take care of me, bitch! Get the fuckin' story right; I don't want Cyrus! That nigga will forever be in love with the Koko but ain't shit happening on this end. And for the muthafuckin' record, I do have a card without a limit. The difference between me and her, my name is on my shit; not Cyrus'."

"Koko—"

Jackie hit the wall with a thud after she was punched hard in the face. Koko kept hitting her until she drew blood. Cyrus' baby mama didn't want the ass whooping Koko was dishing out because she didn't say nor do anything to help. Jackie, on the other hand, was getting the business and couldn't do anything to stop the haymakers Koko was throwing at her. Sheree ran out of the bathroom to get help without either one of the women noticing.

"Baby girl, let her go. This is not worth going to jail for." A deep baritone accompanied by a pair of strong arms whispered in Koko's ear. The man was able to pry Koko off of Jackie then carried her out of the bathroom.

"My purse and shoes are in there! Put me down," Koko yelled. "I can't get home without my damn keys!"

The guy stopped briefly then turned to someone. "Go back in there and get her shoes and purse. Bring them outside. I'll be waiting in the lot."

Bad as she wanted to punch the strange man in his back until he put her down, Koko thought better of it because the muscles in his arms could snap her neck in one swift movement. He moved through the venue at top speed as people looked on trying to figure out what happened. Koko looked up in time to see Austin standing with a smirk on his face with his phone to his ear.

Koko knew Austin was giving Cyrus a play-by-play, but she didn't give a damn what was said. She would bet big money he didn't utter a vowel about spilling the tea on what Cyrus had done behind her back. Austin was a bitch and Koko couldn't care less because all of them could suck her ass through a straw. In the meantime, she had to get away from the man whose cologne was causing her pussy to purr uncontrollably.

Chapter 4

Kazimir St. Claire walked out of the men's restroom drying his hands as he made his way back to the center of the venue. He traveled from Chicago to Minnesota to kick it with his homie Larenz "Lowkey" Murphy and see how he was getting down in the world of entrepreneurship. From the looks of it, Lowkey was doing the damn thing. He had celebrities bringing the people out and money in his pockets. Kaz, as his close friends called him, was proud. With Nelly in the building, the women were deep and that brought the men out to admire the eye candy from afar or to take one or two away with them for the night.

As he walked down the hall a commotion from the women's bathroom caught his attention. It sounded like a real-life Royal Rumble coming from behind the door. Kaz was hesitant to enter the place that was usually off limits to men but he had to put a stop to what was going on inside the room. He expected to see a group of women fighting for their lives. That wasn't the case at all. Kaz was utterly surprised to witness a thick chocolate beauty handling her business alone. Feeling like a creep as he admired his ass while she stood ten toes down in the small space.

After a few minutes Kaz sprang into action. It took several attempts to pry baby girl's hands from the other woman's hair. That didn't stop the blows she continued to throw with the left. Once Kaz succeeded in stopping the one-woman brawl, he tossed the feisty fighter over his shoulder then made his exit. There was a small crowd outside the bathroom, but Kaz made his way through without pausing. He spotted Lowkey and gave him a head nod indicating he had everything under control. Lowkey went toward the restrooms after nodding back.

More people were talking amongst themselves probably speculating about what transpired with questionable stares as Kaz moved toward the door. One person caught baby girl's attention and she went off trying to get out of his arms.

"Austin, fuck you with your lame ass! Tell that nigga about your shiesty ways too. Snake muthafucka!"

Without thinking, Kaz tapped Koko on the ass before scolding her softly. "What you not gon' do is give that nigga the attention he's seeking. Let him do whatever he feels fit. You're better than that. You kill these pussy muthafuckas with kindness," he said, pushing the door open with more force than intended.

Treading across the parking lot heated, Kaz didn't like when sistas were angry in public because it was partially the reason they were labeled "angry black women". Plus, it was unattractive to him. Kaz didn't believe the woman he saved from a criminal charge was problematic. Something was said or done to set her off. Placing her on the hood of his vehicle, Kaz stood in front of her silently.

The *Paco Rabanne Phantom* perfume she wore had him in a trance. Kaz was familiar with the scent, but it radiated off her body differently. He took a deep breath and his eyes closed instantly. The sound of baby girl's voice snapped him back to the woman sitting before him.

"No disrespect, but don't ever—"

Kaz placed his finger to her lips, cutting off the rant he was sure to come. The expression on her face was one of shock. Koko opened her mouth and Kaz shook his head. "You are a Queen. Don't ever bow down to peasants. Your crown tilted tonight but I was there to straighten that muthafucka for you. From this day forth, I want you to never

50

allow anyone to take you back to a place of lowering your standards."

Koko had no clue who the man was, but he said some real shit that had her thinking. He was absolutely correct. Jackie and Cyrus made Koko revert back to the old her. She had left that side of her in Chicago. The deception from folks who were supposed to love her flipped a switch activating the demon inside. Taking everything the mystery man said in, Koko ignored the fact of him putting his finger on her mouth on top of cutting off what she wanted to say.

The entire time he spoke, Koko admired his dark skin, wavy fade with a sharp lining, a mustache connecting to his thick beard which was well groomed around a set of succulent lips. She loved a well-dressed man who had compassion for a woman. If emojis appeared in a person's eyes when they felt emotions, Koko would have heart shaped pupils. The Lance Gross look-a-like had her in a chokehold.

"Lil mama, are you hearing what I'm saying to you? Seriously, it seems as if this shit went in one ear and out the other. I don't like to be ignored, jo."

Koko smirked because he was sexy as hell as he crossed his arms over his chest. She glanced down taking in the way his legs were spread apart showcasing his bowed legs. Adjusting her position on the car, Koko looked up at him once more.

"First and foremost, my name is not lil mama, shawty, nor baby girl. It's Kameeko, but everybody calls me Koko unless its business," she said licking her lips. "I heard every word you said and I appreciate you for reminding me how far I have come in life. What happened back there isn't who I am anymore but I would dish out another ass whoopin' if needed. One thing I won't stand back and do is allow someone to play in my face."

Thinking about why she reacted the way she did, Koko became angry all over again. Seeing her mood change, Kaz lifted her chin with his finger. Koko was beautiful to him and he wanted to see her smile instead of scowling.

"You're too beautiful to be frowning. That shit causes wrinkles." Koko laughed as she tried to hide the fact she was blushing. "There's the smile I was waiting for."

"Who are you?" she asked leaning back on her hands. "You don't sound like you're from here."

"My name is Kazimir. You're right, I'm not from here. I'm from…"

"Chicago," both of them said in unison.

"How did you know that?" he quizzed.

"When you called me jo early. You have to be from the Chi to pick up on that."

"So, you from Chicago too?"

"Born and raised. I just had to leave the nest and find myself. I ended up here and after four years, I'm ready to move the fuck on."

"Kameeko, I know damn well you not going to allow anyone to run you away from here."

"Correction, I have too much to lose. If I stay, everything I've worked hard for will be taken away because I'll be in jail. Trust me."

"This state is big enough to get lost in. There's a way for you to avoid whatever and whomever to continue what you've achieved. It's all about knowing how far ahead you are of the bullshit. Remember, you are the Queen of your world." Kaz sincerely stated. "Have you thought about going back to Chicago?"

He watched as Koko thought about his question. A sense of sadness shadowed over her face, making Kaz believe she had a deeper story to tell. Koko pushed off the car without answering and ran toward the club causing Kaz to scoop her into his arms for the second time that night. Fumbling in his pockets, he removed the keys to his vehicle and hit the button on the fob to unlock the doors. Kaz opened the door sitting Koko in the driver seat before he closed it behind her.

He looked in the direction Koko was headed and spotted the woman she was fighting in the bathroom. While Kaz was focused elsewhere, Koko climbed over the console and jumped out of the car on the passenger side. "Jackie, come here. Let me holla at you," she yelled across the parking lot. "I wasn't finished fuckin' you up, bitch!"

Jackie stopped in her tracks as she followed the voice of her friend. When she spotted Koko walking briskly in her direction, Jackie took a few steps backwards but still opened her mouth to say something slick. "Koko, your beef is with Cyrus, not me. He's the one who had a baby on you. It was he that lied to you but you're mad at me. Yeah, okay." Jackie laughed. "I told your stupid ass to leave him long ago. You didn't listen, so that's on you."

"And this ass whoppin' on me too,' Koko said running toward her.

By the time Jackie got to the entrance of the club, Koko was dragging her back to the parking lot by the hair. She was on Jackie like flies on shit. Kaz took his time getting to them in order to break up the fight because he felt Jackie earned the right to get beat up after laughing at Koko's pain. Jackie didn't stand a chance of getting a scratch in the way Koko dragged her along the pavement. Another female stepped in and hit her in the back of the head. Koko release Jackie and went to town on her too. Koko was handling her ass like a true Chicagoan. Koko punched ol' girl so hard she fell backwards. Kaz jogged over the moment Koko started stomping her head into the concrete.

He had to push his way through the small crowd that gathered around them and pulled Koko away. Jackie used that opportunity to get one last hit in smacking Koko in the face. Koko cackled as she fought to get out of Kaz's grasp.

"Let me go!" Koko demanded. "If she hit me one more time, I'm kickin' yo' ass next," she snarled at Kaz.

"No, you not. You already got the best of both of them, Kameeko. It's over."

Lowkey walked up to Kaz with a pair of heels and a purse in his hand. "Take her home, fam. This shit is bringing too much heat to my establishment."

"I don't know her like that, but I will make sure she leaves the premises."

"I'll get off your property on my own. I don't need an escort. But tell yo' bitch, every time I see her, I'm taggin' that ass! Get ready to drop a bag on cosmetic surgery because she's gonna need it." Koko snatched her items from Lowkey then glanced up at Kaz. "You gon' let me go? I'm done with this shit."

Kaz didn't believe a word that came out of her mouth because Jackie was still talking crazy loud enough for her to hear. One word could set Koko off and Kaz was not in the mood to be wrestling with her feisty ass anymore. He removed his arms from around Koko's waist but held on to her hand. Koko twisted her hand away and reached into her purse. She pulled a ticket out and walked across the lot.

"Did you drive, or do you need a ride?"

"I parked in valet. Thanks for your help, but I got it from here."

Kaz grabbed her arm before turning Koko to look at him. The tears falling down her face did something to his heart. Pain was on full display and it told Kaz whatever started the beef between Koko and her friend hurt her deeply.

"I can't allow you to drive in the condition you're in. Hop in the car with me and we can talk about what's on your mind."

"I'm fine, Kazimir. I don't know you, and going anywhere with you is out of the question. What I'm dealing with is now in the past. I've learned niggas ain't shit and so-called friends ain't either. Like I said before, thank you for your help. I'll be fine in due time."

54

Koko walked away without another word and Kaz couldn't do anything except allow her to go. Whoever the guy was that hurt her had fucked it up for another man to show her what real love was about. Kaz wanted to run behind her and put his number in her phone so she could call him anytime, but he wasn't sure if she would accept the friendship so, he walked away and let her be.

***

Entering his hotel suite in downtown Minneapolis, Kaz kicked off his shoes with Kameeko still on his mind. He waited until she was seated in her vehicle and drove away before he did the same. Kameeko was either being taken care of by her ex, or she was doing very well for herself. He wondered how she allowed a man to have her acting out the way he witnessed at the club. There was so much more to her and Kaz was eager to find out. In his mind he knew fate was real and if it was meant to be, he and Kameeko would cross paths again.

As he undressed to shower, Kaz's phone rang on the bed where he had thrown it. Glancing at his watch, it was two in the morning. There was only one person who would call him at that time. Taking a deep breath, he answered and put the call on speaker.

"What's up, Nicolette?"

"When are you coming home, Kazimir? Alessia and I miss you."

"Save the bullshit for somebody else. You and I both know I'm the last person you miss. What do you want?"

"See, this is what I've been talking about. It's been two years and you still can't get with the program. You're my husband, Kazimir!"

"On paper, Nicolette. On paper. I never agreed to be your husband. That shit was forced upon me so, I did what I had to do in order to help my grandfather. Stop acting like you didn't know about the arrangement. This marriage is fake as a counterfeit bill."

"We are legally married and it's time for you to act like it. I don't care how we were brought together. In the state of Illinois, I am Nicolette St. Clair and you are my husband. And while we're at it, when are you going to sign Alessia's birth certificate? She's two for Christ sakes! She needs you as her father, Kazimir!"

Kaz sighed as he stepped out of his pants. He was tired of having the same conversation with Nicolette. She only got in her feelings when he was out of town. Any time he was in Chicago, none of the shit came up.

"Are you with a woman?"

"If I was, there would be nothing you could do about it now, is there? Nicolette, I'll be back in Chicago sometime tomorrow. Just keep telling your nosy ass friends I'm out of town on business. Go to sleep," Kaz said ending the call.

Sitting on the edge of the bed, Kaz ran his hand down his face. He was dreading going back to the house he shared with his wife Nicolette. Kaz never imagined he would be married at the age of twenty-six to a woman he wasn't in love with. Things you do for the ones you love could be insane. There was nothing Kaz wouldn't do for the one who raised him to be the man he was today. The only thing he couldn't do was pretend to be happy.

At the age of twelve, Kaz was living the life of luxury with his mama and daddy on the south side of Chicago. Kellan "Kelo" St. Clair was kingpin of the Chi who ran the city with the purest dope around. Kaz wanted for nothing growing up. He had the latest gear, gaming systems, and all the sneakers a preteen could ever wear in a lifetime. There was always food in the refrigerator and all his friends were at his house to eat good too. His mother Simona St. Claire didn't mind the company Kaz kept because she loved to look after the ones who were less fortunate than others. She drew the line at him spending time at his friend's homes because she was afraid of something happening to her one and only child.

Being on the A honor roll earned Kaz everything he had received from his parents. He made sure to make them proud. They took him on trips out of the country every summer, and he was able to choose the destination he wanted to visit for his birthday. Kaz had been to more places than the average adult, thanks to his folks. It wasn't all about going places all the time for Kaz. He also loved to spend time with his Grandfather Paxton St. Claire.

Pax as he was called was a prestigious businessman who owned a candy factory in the heart of downtown Chicago. Kaz used to be his taste taster whenever his paw-paw created a new flavor of candy. The summers he spent with Pax were the ones he looked forward to. Learning about the business was more exciting to him than splashing around in the ocean. Kaz wanted to be just like his granddad one day and he worked hard so he could achieve that.

In 2010, Kaz was learning the ends and outs of making hard candy when he was approached by Pax. He had a somber expression on his face as he stood before his grandson. Kaz's hands started shaking uncontrollably because he knew something bad had happened. The tears in Pax's eyes said it all.

"Kaz, we have to go. It's Kellan and Simona."

"They dead, ain't they?"

Pax nodded and a tear dropped from his eyes. Kaz didn't show any emotion after hearing the news. Kelo, had already prepared his son in the event of something happening to him. Kaz was always told the line of work his father was in could be dangerous. He also told Kaz he would always be taken care of in his absence. Everything Kaz would need was locked away in a safe underneath the floorboard in his bedroom closet. He was given specific order to contact Kelo's lawyer the day of his demise and not to breathe a word of it to Pax.

Kaz felt guilty holding information from his paw-paw, but he gave his word and Kaz was going to honor that. His loyalty had always been with his father, but at the moment, he felt some type of way because his mother was caught in the line of fire with him. In Kaz's mind, his father preached how he was the provider and protector of his family, but he wasn't able to protect the woman he loved.

"Come on, Kazimir. I'm taking you home with me. David will stay with you while I go take care of your parent's final arrangements," Pax said hugging his grandson. "It's okay to cry, son. I got you from this day forth."

The ride to Pax's home was quiet giving Kaz time to think about how his life was about to change without his parents. The image of his mother and the sound of her voice echoed in his mind continuously. Kaz was wide awake but the scenery outside the vehicle wasn't what he saw. He smelled the salt of the beautiful bluish green ocean of Aruba. It was the last place his family vacationed two weeks prior. The smile on his mother's face was all Kaz saw because he had the same image saved in his phone.

Kaz got up and went to the mini bar to pour up a much-needed drink. Reminiscing about how he ended up in a whole marriage took him back to the worst day of his life. With the help of his father's lawyer, Kaz was able to get everything Kelo left for his only son. He didn't learn the dynamics of his parent's death until he graduated high school at the age of eighteen. Kaz left Chicago to attend the University of North Carolina. The Tarheels were his father's favorite college basketball team and Kaz wanted to wear the jersey in his honor. He spent a lot of his time in the backyard learning the game whenever his dad was home. In his absence, Kaz practiced every chance he got so he could get closer to winning the next time he and Kelo stepped on the court.

Kaz played on the varsity team all through high school and earned a full ride to college not only for academics, but also for basketball. The money his father put aside for his schooling went to Kaz's bank account along with the millions that were put into a trust. Even though he was well off, Kaz still played the role of a struggling student throughout his college years. During that time, he became the man in North Carolina without having to get his hands dirty. Being a drug dealer wasn't something Kaz wanted to do because his father always told him to go big or go home in everything he did. Selling drugs was something neither one of his parents wanted him to indulge in, but shit happened.

After being entered into the NBA draft, Kaz had to get out the game so he didn't have dirt on his name once he turned pro. He turned his empire over to his right-hand man Steelo, but still had his hand somewhat in the pot. Playing pro ball was put on hold when Kaz received a call from his paw-paw to come home. With no questions asked, Kaz got on the first thing smoking back to Chicago.

Pax had a car waiting for his grandson at the airport which took him straight to his home in Plainfield, Illinois. It had been years since Kaz had been to the mansion his grandfather had built from the ground up when he turned fifteen years old. St. Claire Candies was a multimillion-dollar business Pax started on his own. Kaz didn't get into his grandfather's affairs but that day, he wished he'd been on top of the books instead of David. Kaz had dual degrees in both Accounting and Business. David, on the other hand, was giving the job because he was Pax's son.

Soon as Kaz entered the house he became pissed. Pax was the type of man who didn't like a dirty home. Walking into the entryway, it appeared the house hadn't been dusted in Lord knows how long. When he stepped foot into the living room, there were alcohol bottles, clothes, and ashtrays with cigarette and blunts stubbed out in them. The place looked like an expensive ass trap house. Kaz couldn't believe what he was seeing and wondered where the hell were the maids paw-paw had on his payroll.

The pungent stench throughout the lower level of the house had Kaz's stomach turning. He moved slowly toward the kitchen praying he didn't find a dead body on the other side of the island. It definitely smelled like there was one close by. When Kaz stepped into the kitchen there were dishes everywhere. It looked like the kitchen hadn't been cleaned in months. There was grease and dirty pots and pans with old oil and food still in them. Shaking his head, Kaz left to find his grandfather hoping he ran into David along the way.

Damn near running upstairs two at a time, Kaz stood outside Pax's bedroom door taking a deep breath before entering. The sight before him almost brought him to his knees. Pax laid in bed watching the news. He looked up and smiled.

"Kellan, I knew you would come. How have you been, son?"

Kaz's heart almost stopped because in just six months his grandfather's health had taken a turn for the worse. Pax suffered a heart attack and a stroke which brought Kaz back home to make sure he had the medial help he would need. He wasn't informed of anything else happening after that timeframe. It had to be something more going on because there has never been a moment Pax had ever mistaken him for his father.

"Paw-paw, it's me, Kazimir."

Pax shift his eyes back to the television before giving his attention back to Kaz. "That's what I meant. How you doing?"

"I'm fine but I have a question of my own. What's going on with you? The house is a mess, you are about fifty pounds lighter, and on top of that, you didn't know who I was when I entered this room."

"It's nothing."

"Don't tell me it's nothing when I know there's a lot of shit going on that I don't know about!" Kaz snapped. *"What happened to the maid service?"*

"Kazimir, take a seat, son. You're right. I have been holding a lot from you because worrying you about my life was something I didn't want to do. You have so much going on for yourself and I don't want to be a burden."

"No matter what I have going on, you are my top priority, paw-paw. If something happens to you, I wouldn't know what I'd do. So, please, stop beating around the bush and tell me what's been happening."

Kaz took a seat on the side of the bed and his grandfather moved over to give him more room. Pax stalled as he fought to remember what he was about to say. The frustration in his face let Kaz know he was having a difficult time getting his wording together. Being as patient as he could, Kaz waited while taking in his grandfather's features. Even though Pax was in his late seventies, he looked very sickly. Kaz remembered when his grandfather was fit and in shape. The person lying in the bed was far from being healthy.

"Kazimir, after my last stay in the hospital, I was diagnosed with early signs of dementia. I tend to forget a lot of things and it's hard at times. David took on the role of being my caretaker and fired the help. He promised he would make sure everything around the house were taken care of. Obviously, from what you just said, he hasn't been keeping up his end of the bargain."

Kaz glanced around the bedroom and it was much cleaner than the rest of the home.

"I haven't been out of the bed in months and David makes sure I'm fed and my bedroom is spotless. I assumed he was taking care of the rest of the house as well. My health is declining, Kazimir. I called you here because I need your help. My business was going under—"

"What do you mean your business is going under? Pax, your company makes millions. There's no way it should be failing."

"As you know, I put David in charge of the finances. He hasn't been keeping up with the books and I had to reach out for outside help."

Kaz was baffled about what Pax said and couldn't believe it. His grandfather had enough money to last a lifetime, but he was saying he was damn near broke. How? Kaz didn't have a say so in the matter when David took over the accounting position back in the day because he was too young to understand. At that point, he knew his uncle had driven his grandfather's business into the ground.

"No, paw-paw, you don't have to do that. How much do you need? I have money and can help you." Kaz said, positioning himself on the bed. *"I didn't tell you years ago, but my father made sure I would be well taken care of if something happened to him."*

"I know that already, Kaz. Your father was a great man and always took care of his responsibilities. He just couldn't bring that drug shit around me. I didn't want his dirty money then, and I don't want it now."

"Pax, you are talking crazy right now. That money is cleaner than a baby's ass. It no longer belongs to Kellan, it's mine! Now, how much do you need?"

"I've already made a deal with Anthony Santoro."

Kaz didn't know who the fuck that was, but the name alone sounded janky to him. He put the name in his memory so he could dig into him a little deeper when he could. Pax may have put himself in a jam that he wasn't in any position to get out of. The thought of it had Kaz hotter than the devil's den.

"What did you agree to, paw-paw? This Anthony character sounds like a loan shark."

"He's not a loan shark. Mr. Santoro helped save my company and he gave me two years to pay his money back.

That's a piece of cake. I'll have it paid off before the timeframe."

"Paw-paw, I need to see the contract so I can read it over. And where is David?"

Just as Kaz asked about his uncle, he walked into the bedroom. Standing from the bed, Kaz had the look of death in his eyes as he studied David up and down. The house looked ran down and his ass was dressed in designer from head to toe, draping in jewelry. For him to be forty-eight years old, one would think he was a young nigga who was getting money on the block.

"You're out in the streets dressed down in Balenciaga while my grandfather's business is struggling financially, and he had to go to another muthafucka for money. What the fuck have you been doing?"

"Lil nigga, who the fuck do you think you are questioning me? I've been the one here taking care of his ass while you were away being the star on the basketball court."

"Is that what you call what you're doing? The way this house looks you ain't been doing shit except spending all his money. Not to mention, paw-paw looks malnourished. Are you even here to feed him? I know you're not cooking because the stove doesn't appear to have been used in forever."

"He's dying! He is in the early stages of dementia and he also has stage four liver cancer. There's nothing more the doctors can do to help him. He refused chemo and radiation. My father was given six months to live last week. What do you want me to do when he refuses to eat; force feed him? All I can do is wait for the day he dies so I can bury him."

Kaz haul off and punched his uncle in the mouth. He didn't appreciate the way he talked down on Pax's condition. David hit the floor after Kaz hit him with a left and right hook, followed by an uppercut. He could hear Pax yelling for him to stop. He didn't cease the assault until he heard his grandfather struggling to catch his breath. When Kaz turned to make sure he was okay, he witnessed him clutching his chest.

"Paw-paw, hold on!" Kaz said, snatching his phone from his pocket to call 911.

After giving the dispatcher the address, he got into the bed and cradled his grandfather until help arrived. David on the other hand had gotten his ass off the floor and left without a care. There was so much Kaz wanted to ask Pax but the time was not right. All he wanted was to get him to the hospital so he wouldn't die.

Fate was on Pax's side because he survived the second heart attack and his cancer was in remission. All thanks to his grandson. Kaz kicked David out of the house and moved in to take care of his paw-paw. Even though his uncle was removed from Pax's personal space, he was still the accountant of the company. That was why Kaz had to ultimately marry Anthony Santoro's granddaughter, Nicolette two years later at the age of twenty-four.

Santoro was going to allow Kaz to pay off the debt then renege when he found out his daughter was pregnant. In return for the payback, Santoro wanted Kaz to marry Nicolette and raise the baby as his own. Kaz refused and told him he had the money his grandfather owed. Santoro in return told Kaz if he didn't go through with the plan, Pax would be dead by morning. Kaz had no choice but to go through with the wedding. One thing he didn't do was legally commit to being the father of Nicolette's daughter Alessia.

Aleesia was innocent in the whole situation. Kaz had been in her life since she was a week old and had him wrapped around her finger. She would forever be Kaz's baby girl, but Nicolette wasn't going to force him to put that shit in writing. The shots of bourbon had him feeling good, but his thoughts had drained all the energy out of him. Taking a shower was not part of his plan once he fell back on the mattress. Koko took over his mind guiding Kaz into a deep sleep dreaming about holding her in his arms.

Chapter 5

"Hey, Horace, how you doing?"

Koko was at the studio after taking a couple days to get her head back in the game. She was behind on her previous project and had to call for reinforcement. There was money to be made and a dusty muthafucka wasn't going to stop her from getting to it.

"Koko! I'm good. You need me?"

"Damn, is it that obvious?" She chuckled. "I feel bad for calling now."

"Don't you ever feel bad about calling me. Whenever you need me; I'll be there." Horace sang in his best Michael Jackson voice. "All jokes aside though; what you need?"

"I have a big project I need you to assist me with. As a bonus, you can be my plus one at the event too. It's in Chicago. Are you down for a road trip?"

"Hell yeah! I heard it's rough in the Windy City. All I ask is for you to take me to O'block. I need a thug in my life."

"Fool, I'm from there and I don't go on 63rd and King Drive. That's for sure out of the question. Get here when you can because I'm not about to even make you think there's another like King Von in Chicago."

"See, you tripping. It's okay. Go 'head and hold out on all the big dick niggas. I'm not mad, but I'm upset you don't want me to be happy."

"Get off my phone, Horace. I got work to do."

"Okay, boo. I'll be there within the hour."

Koko shook her head laughing at the silliness of Horace Macabee. She met him within the first year she moved to Minnesota. Scrolling on social media to find a popular club, she happened on a post about a spot called *Gay 90's* in downtown Minneapolis. It was a gay club but she knew they were the people to party with without the drama. Koko went out alone to enjoy the nightlife in a new city and she was not disappointed. It was a little awkward at first because there were a lot of lesbians eyeballing her with lustful stares. She didn't mind long as they didn't approach her on a level she wasn't down with.

Standing on the wall bobbing her head, Koko nursed the drink she held in her hand while watching everyone around her have a good time. The music was on point and she knew soon as she met some people to vibe with, the club would be one she frequented often. A tall man wearing a pink t-shirt with the word *Slay* printed in bold rainbow colors on the front, white straight legged pants, and a pair of pink Coach sneakers on his feet kept looking in her direction. The man was very handsome and groomed to perfection. His manicured nails looked better than most women. He had a soft muscular build and seemed to carry himself well to Koko. His eyebrows were arched, he wore lip gloss, and the pink coach bag matched his shoes down to the color. He made his way over and stopped right in front of Koko.

Leaning forward to whisper in her ear, "You gon' hold up the wall all night? There's a time to be had here, hunni. Let me show you how to have a good time."

Without giving Koko a minute to protest, she was dragged to the dance floor where they stay the duration of the night. A friendship was developed in a matter of hours and Koko was glad she gave Horace a chance to show her how they had fun in the Twin Cities. The two of them have been tight since that night.

Koko was the type of person who always wanted to look out for her people. She brought Horace into her business and taught him everything she knew. He was out of work at the time and took her up on the offer to help when she needed his assistance. With her business rising, Koko had to have a discussion about bringing Horace onboard full-time because it would make finishing a project so easier and she needed his help.

Koko sat her phone on the table next to her working station and walked across the room to wash her hands. She got back to work still thinking about Horace and his crazy antics. After putting the finishing touches on the tiger project, Koko stepped back smiling as she observed her work. If no one was proud of her, she damn sure was. Clapping for a job well done, the bell sounded. Soon as Koko turned to see who was there, her mood changed drastically. Cyrus stood on the other side of the door looking pitiful. She walked across the room then hesitantly turned the lock for him to enter.

"What's up?" Koko asked leaning against the wall.

"How you doing?"

Rolling her eyes, Koko huffed loudly. "Cut the shit, Cyrus. You truly don't give a fuck about me and I've accepted it. Now, why are you here?"

"That's far from the truth. I love you and forever will." Cyrus reached out to grab her hand and Koko sidestepped away from him. "I can't touch you now?"

"Nope. You have a whole baby mama for that. By the way, how's those lumps coming along for her?" she smirked.

"I wanted to holla at you about that."

"There you go! Get to the real reason you showed up. You came to discuss Willie lump lump." Koko laughed. "As a matter of fact, I'll set shit straight. The bitch tried to save a hoe and fucked around and found out. My qualm was with Jackie. She should've sat her ass out of it."

"Why were you and Jackie fighting? Y'all like sisters, man."

"We *were* like sisters! The shit I heard her saying to your baby mama was fucked up. I would've respected the bitch had she told the truth. But she tried to make me out to be a bum ass bitch who needed you. Jackie was the main one who I allowed to eat with me plenty of days and she was plotting on me the entire time. I'm cool on that because I could've killed her in that damn bathroom and again outside the club."

Cyrus stood quietly as he took in what Koko said. Jackie and Sheree told a different story. He believed the woman he considered his. One thing for sure, Cyrus knew Koko didn't like drama. She tried her best to avoid it at all costs. So, for her to physically put her hands on both of them, he should've known there was more to it. Cyrus initially came to curse her out but Koko set him straight without stuttering. The hurt in her eyes let him know he had lost the love of his life. Cyrus had one question to ask before he left.

"Who was the nigga carrying you through the club?"

Koko scoffed folding her arms over her chest. Cyrus didn't have the right to question her about anything after all he'd put her through. She decided not to dwell on the past because it was no longer her problem. Plus, his actions opened her eyes to the bullshit he was on and Koko was prepared to walk away without looking back.

"You in my business, Cyrus. Be happy he was able to get me off your wack-ass friend and baby mama. Otherwise, you would be raising your son alone while making funeral arrangements for his mama."

"Nah, that's not answering my question. Who is he, Koko? Austin already told me how the nigga was smackin' you on yo' ass and shit. Stop playing with me before you piss me off," Cyrus snarled.

Koko laughed hysterically in his face. Wiping the tears from her eyes, Cyrus was furious at her reaction. She didn't care how he felt because he was going to feel lower than the floor he was standing on when she made him feel every word that came out of her mouth.

"You listening to Austin now? The same Austin who sat next to me that night telling me how you weren't shit for cheating on me? The muthafucka who thought disclosing how many bitches you had coming through on the block, huh? Let me not forget to mention him spilling the tea about you having a child as if it was a flex. Hell, if I didn't know about Cj, Austin's bitch ass would've blown your spot all the way up. I'd advise you to reevaluate the company you keep. If he can flap his lips to me about your wrongdoings, his ass would do the same with the Feds. If I was gullible, Austin would've been able to shoot his shot in the process and I would've fell for it. But I'm a real bitch. I don't fuck a nigga's friend behind his back."

Cyrus stepped toward her with his fists clenched tightly. He bit down on his bottom lip as if he was trying hard not to say anything in response to what Koko said. Cyrus had plans to check Austin soon as he was in his presence again. He shouldn't have been telling his business to anybody. Especially not to Koko.

"I don't care what Austin told you. I want to know who was feeling you up for everybody to see."

"What are you going to do, hit me?" Koko asked unfazed. "If that's what you're on we can tear this muthafucka up because a punching bag is something I will not become. The damage would definitely get fixed; I'm insured."

"Have I ever put my hands on you violently? Choking your ass while my dick is deep in your guts don't count." Cyrus said as he waited for Koko to respond. When she didn't, he continued. "Exactly, the answer is no. So, don't come at me like that."

"I mean, you're the one who walked up on me with aggressive testosterone levels," she said pushing past him. "I'm not answering your question. Don't ask again."

"Oh, you gon' answer! You owe me that much, Koko!"

Koko spun around angrily. "I don't owe you shit!" she said pointing her finger at him. "If anything, you owe me for the love I gave unconditionally while you put conditions on yours. Don't get me started on the loyalty I showed openly and privately from the beginning. Even with the bitches and snake niggas laughing at my stupidity. We not gon' forget about the endless pussy I gave your ass not knowing the sensual strokes weren't just for me. Cyrus, like I told Jackie, fuck you!"

Tears ran down Koko's face because she was mad at herself for staying with Cyrus long as she did. Had she left after seeing the first red flag, Koko wouldn't be showing her emotions in that moment. Koko had to let out how she really felt and hopefully, Cyrus would leave her alone.

"We were together for years and not once did I feel our relationship was growing to the next level. Hell, we lived separately the entire time and now the shit makes sense. You didn't want to solely commit to living together because then you would've had to lie and sneak your way out of the house." Koko chuckled.

"Putting more effort in my business kept my mind off what was really going on between us. The shit is smacking me in the face now that I'm thinking about it in depth. That only shows I was suppressing the situation maybe in hopes things would get better. Silly me, huh? What's ironic is, you never complained about the time we weren't spending together while I was working. To hear Jackie disclose all you're doing for the bitch you had a baby with had me feeling some type of way. Not that I needed anything from you, but how the fuck she gets a house with all expenses paid, and a fucking black card? Hell, I borrow money from you and you looking for that shit back!" She chuckled. "Don't worry; it's cool."

Cyrus' lack of concern when it came to Koko was there all along. Her heart helped her ignore every bit of it. Love was a powerful tool that could blind Stevie Wonder for a second time. Glancing over Cyrus' body Koko cringed at his sagging jeans, obnoxious amount of jewelry, and the cigarette behind his ear. He never smoked around her because he knew how much Koko hated the smell of his addiction choice. Kazimir entered her mind and she wished she had given him the time of day when the chance arose. He was the definition of a man who had his affairs in order. Too bad she missed the opportunity.

"Contrary to what you believe, I do love you. Our relationship is strong as fuck. We're locked in, Koko."

"Strong for who? You? The only thing we have is a strong sexual connection. Hell, I'm second guessing that too. If it was important, other bitches wouldn't have been able to get the same treatment. For the record, *we're* not locked in anymore. It's a wrap."

Cyrus paced back and forth across the room in deep thought. Koko checked her apple watch because at that point Cyrus was wasting her time. She wanted to have things in place once Horace arrived.

"Anytime we have a disagreement we patch that shit up and move forward. What's different now?" Cyrus had the gall to ask.

"I'm tired of not being enough for you. If I'm going to be in a one-sided relationship I may as well date myself. To be frank, I've been doing just that for some time. In fact, I support myself in everything I've ever done, I provide for me, pay my own bills in my own place, I take myself on dates, and I even fuck myself when you are out doing who knows what. So, why would I continue to be an option?"

"You fucked that nigga! How long have you been creeping with him?" Cyrus bellowed out.

"When I fuck *him* or anyone else, you will be the first to know. Get out of my place of business, Cyrus. I have work to do. This conversation is over."

"I'm going to leave before I say something I'll regret later." Cyrus turned to leave but he didn't open the door. Instead, he stood with his back to her with his head held down. "Koko, I will always love you. I'm sorry for everything we've been through. I never meant to hurt you." he turned to face her with tears in his eyes.

"We will get back together, have kids, and get married. For now, I'm going to fall back. Be good, baby. You are my future and it won't be easy to watch you walk out of my life for good."

Cyrus left before Koko could tell him what he said was wishful thinking. Horace rushed in and straight to his friend. When the tears fell from her eyes, he wrapped his arms tightly around her and allowed Koko to cry out her pain. The sound of her sobs pissed Horace off.

"We have so much to catch up on, I see. For his sake, I hope he didn't put his hands on you. At the end of the day, I'm still a man. Cyrus can get his ass whooped."

***

The day had come for Koko to head to Chicago. On one hand she was excited to present the replica locomotive she created for the event, but on the other, she was dreading being in the same city she left behind for peace. Not only was the city in turmoil and frightened Koko to return to the crime that had worsened throughout the years, but her own personal trauma played a major role in how she felt as well. She hadn't seen her family in four years and had no plans of doing so during her visit. The trip was all about getting her name out there and getting to the bag. Koko felt the project was going to put her on the map for any and every one to seek her out for their customized ideas that she could put into edible sweetness.

Koko was excited to get on the road. She watched as the movers she hired to transport her work to Chicago made sure everything was secured inside. The refrigerated truck she purchased was loaded up along with the small extras she created on her own. Horace pulled up and it was time for them to head out. The drive was going to be a long one. Seven hours at least.

"Koko, I brought some snacks and drinks so we can get through this ride joyfully. My playlist is ready, weed is on deck—"

"Aht, aht. There will be no smoking," Koko interjected.

"Come on now, boo. I will not survive without my trees! You have to make an exception this one time. Please don't deprive me of this."

Horace was pleading for his weed sessions in Koko's presence and she felt bad because he looked so sad while doing so. She didn't allow anyone to smoke anything around her; not even Cyrus. Horace was right though; we did have a long ride ahead of us.

"This is what we can do. You can smoke long as you roll down the window and blow it out. What I will not allow is you flaming up the entire ride. I won't be able to handle that much."

"Girl, you act like I need some type of help or something," Horace chuckled. "I'm going to respect your boundaries, boo. I appreciate the fact of you even allowing me to smoke. Now, what's the plan?"

"I have no problem driving the whole way, but you can take over whenever you like. I won't complain," Koko replied. "The drivers already have the address to the venue. All we have to do is be there to make sure the project gets there in one piece and is put away in the walk-in cooler properly. Then we off to the hotel until the party tomorrow night."

"Soooooo, that means we can roll on over to O'block, right?"

"Horace, you can get on the 3 King Drive bus and take yourself. I'll even pay for your fare. Me and my truck are not going over there for you to sightsee. We may not make it back home if we do. We are going to stay our asses downtown and find something safe to do."

"Who is afraid to drive around their own city? That shit sounds weird."

"Me! I'm not going to act like I'm not. I was terrified when I lived there. The fuck you talking about." Koko laughed. "Let me put it like this, you've been to South Minneapolis, right?"

"Of course."

"Well imagine that but larger. Why do you think they call Minneapolis mini-Chicago? The crime rate is horrible. Just like my city; if not worse."

"Koko, you are exaggerating. Stop playing with me."

"I'm not. Again, if you want to go to O'block, you're on your own. Case closed. It's time to go anyway. I hope you bought a suit like I asked you to."

"Why are you insulting my intelligence, Miss Simmons? I will blend in with them rich muthafuckas so well you're going to be looking for me without recognition."

"I can't wait to see it. Get in the car. I'm about to tell the drivers it's time."

Horace did what he was told and soon as he sat in the passenger seat, Koko's phone rang. He didn't want to invade her privacy so he didn't even look down at the device that sat in the cupholder. When it rang a second time, he took the initiative to take a peek. Cyrus name appeared on the screen and he immediately sent the call to voicemail.

The day Horace walked into KoKo Kakes & More and saw his friend crying, the two of them sat down and talked about everything she had been going through. It hurt Horace's heart because he wasn't there for Koko through her trials and tribulations. He always thought there was something off about Jackie but it wasn't his place to say anything to Koko more than once. To hear the things she said made him dislike Jackie more than he already had. For her to call herself Koko's sister, then talk down on her to another was wrong on all levels. Not only that, Koko paid Jackie's rent when she was about to be evicted. Koko even took her on a shopping spree once and also made sure she kept money in her pockets. But to thank her for what she had done, Jackie stabbed Koko in the back and may as well had spit in her face in the process.

"You ready?" Koko asked getting into the vehicle.

"Sure am. Oh, Cyrus called." Horace said going through his playlist on his phone. "You still talking to him?"

"I've talked to him a time or two. No, I'm not going back. I already know that was going to be your next question."

"Koko, we're grown. What you do with your life is yours to do whatever you see fit. I will always be here when you need me. Even if you decide to try to make things work. You and I both know I do not like Cyrus. If your decision is to go back, I will support you in that...from afar." Horace paused.

"I love you with all my heart. But I cannot...let me correct that, I will not stand by and watch him mistreat you. Please leave me out of whatever y'all go through because I don't do episodes. Hit me up with the finale. Our friendship is airtight and will be forever. I just don't want to be in the middle of the back and forth because that shit can be exhausting as hell. You bet not hesitate to tell me if the muthafucka puts his hands on you though."

Koko stared at Horace with a blank expression then reached to push the start button to bring the engine to life in her truck. She was quiet for about two minutes before addressing what Horace said to her. Anyone else would've probably taken offense. Not Koko.

"You didn't have to tell me that but I respect it. Your boundaries are just as important as our friendship. I would never put you in a compromising position to constantly listen to me vent about the things Cyrus would surely put me through again. I had Jackie for that and where did it get me? Never again will I cry to someone then stay and continue to be mistreated. There's no need for you to worry. Thank you for expressing yourself too. Communication is key and I want us to be able to talk about any and everything no matter how much it may hurt."

"I'm with you when you're right. I didn't mean to bring the mood down."

"You didn't. We got that shit out of the way, now it's time for car Karaoke. What are we singing first?" Koko asked.

Loyal by Chris Brown blared through the speakers soon as Horace phone connected. Koko put the gear shift in drive as she bounced to the beat. It was the remix so Lil Wayne was on the track and both of them were ready to spit his verse.

I wasn't born last night
I know these hoes ain't right
But you was blowin' up her phone last night
But she didn't have her ringer nor her ring on last night, ooh
Nigga, that's that nerve
Why give a bitch your heart when she rather have a purse?
Why give a bitch an inch when she rather have nine?
You know how the game goes
She be mine by half time, I'm the shit, ooh
Nigga that's that nerve
You all about her, and she all about hers
Birdman Junior in this bitch, no flamingos
And I done did everything but trust these hoes
When a rich want you
And your nigga can't do nothing for ya
These hoes ain't loyal

Koko sang the chorus with her chest and Cyrus ran through her mind like Shacarri Richardson on the track. She blinked a couple times so she wouldn't go back into the past. She had good intentions to not allow that part of her life to interfere with the future plans she looked forward to. When the song went off, another took its place. Traffic was light so

Koko was easing along the highway smoothly. Horace reached into the back seat and brought a bag forward.

"You want some chips?" he asked.

"No. It's too early for any of that. You didn't eat breakfast?"

"I ate a banana," Horace said opening a bag of chili cheese Fritos. "This will hold me over until we stop to get something to eat."

"We'll find somewhere once we enter Wisconsin. That will be our halfway point to Chicago."

"Sounds good to me."

They seemed to have arrived into Wisconsin quicker than expected and Horace was sleeping his ass off. He drifted off two hours in leaving Koko to entertain herself while driving. She didn't mind at all because the music of H.E.R, Snoh Aalegra, Inayah, Monica, and many others were there to keep her company. Exiting the highway, Koko pulled into a gas station and decided to fill up while she was there.

"Where are we?" Horace asked stretching like a feline.

"Wisconsin. Do me a favor and find a place to eat. Anywhere is cool with me."

"I can do that while I pump the gas and get a quick smoke in."

Koko nodded getting out of the truck. Using her credit card, she inserted it into the slot then Horace took over. He scrolled through his phone deciding on Wendy's to eat. Koko could already taste the double Baconator with a strawberry lemonade to wash it down.

"You chose that spot because it's right there, didn't you?"

"Yep. Why drive around when we can just walk across the lot," Horace shrugged. "I'm eager to get to O'block," he said shaking the nozzle.

"I'm not going back into that conversation. I said what I said about that too many times to count."

Walking off, Koko left Horace where he stood so he could think about the hood by himself. She headed straight for the restroom sign to relieve her bladder. Koko hated using public bathrooms but she didn't have a choice that day. If she wasn't afraid of going to jail, Koko would've gone outside and pissed behind the building. It was probably cleaner than the bathroom she had just walked into. Hurrying to handle her business, she used her foot to flush the toilet and a paper towel to turn the water on at the sink. Holding her breath, Koko washed her hands and damn near ran out of there.

She found Horace already in line at Wendy's. The look on Koko's face instantly put him in protective mode. Soon as she was close enough, Horace was checking her over for signs of assault.

"Whose ass do I need to beat?" he asked lowly.

"Huh?"

"Who is fucking with you, Koko?"

"Nobody. That damn bathroom was nasty as hell but I had to use it. I should've followed my first mind and went behind the building. Maybe I wouldn't feel like bugs are crawling on me now."

"Oh. You had me ready to throw hands. I'm glad it was just a sanitary issue. I know you didn't sit on that toilet."

"Didn't I say it was nasty in there? Hell nawl, I didn't sit on shit. I didn't even touch the handle to turn the water on. Don't insult me, Horace."

The cashier waited until they finished bickering before she called them up to order. Horace ordered a five-dollar meal with a junior bacon cheeseburger, nuggets, fries, and a drink. Koko ordered her double Baconator meal with only lettuce, tomato, cheese, and bacon with a large fry, and a strawberry lemonade. As they waited for their order, Koko found a table for them to sit. Her phone vibrated in her purse soon as she sat down. Removing the device, she saw Cyrus' name on the screen.

"What's up?" Koko asked leaning back against the chair.

"Where are you?"

Pulling the phone from her ear she looked at it as if she had been threatened. Cyrus had to be out of his mind questioning her whereabouts. It wasn't his business where she was.

"I'm minding my business. What's up?" she repeated.

"I wanted to see you, man. You don't have to be nasty about it."

"That's not an option, Cyrus. I'm not even in Minnesota and if I was, we still wouldn't be kickin' it as if we're still together. As a matter of fact, I don't think you should call as much as you've been doing. I'm trying to move on and you are kind of complicating things."

"Move on with who?"

"See what I mean? You have selective hearing right now. Have it ever occurred that I'm moving on for me?"

"It's that nigga, isn't it? He flew yo' ass out to get my pussy, huh?"

Cyrus was yelling into the phone and Koko was over it. She didn't understand how he was so upset about what she did in her life when he didn't appreciate any of that when he was part of the equation. Instead of prolonging the conversation, Koko ended the call. There was no way she was going to allow Cyrus to ruin the mood she was in.

Harace walked over with two trays in each hand and Koko's stomach growled loudly in anticipation for the food she was about to smash. She wasted no time unwrapping the burger and instantly became grossed out. Koko grabbed the burger and headed back to the counter. She waited until someone finally noticed her standing there in wait.

"May I help you?"

"I asked for a Baconator with only lettuce, tomato, cheese, and bacon. This has everything on it. Can someone please make me a sandwich the way I asked for it?"

The cashier walked away and Koko kept her eye on everything going on in the back. As she watched she could see the cashier making her sandwich without gloves. That shit pissed Koko off even more. There was no way she was eating anything somebody made with their bare hands. When the woman returned with the sandwich, she slammed it on the counter as if Koko was to blame for her sandwich being wrong.

"I want a refund. Not now, but right now," Koko said calmly.

"Why do you want a refund all of a sudden? I made the sandwich the way you asked me to do so."

"I agree, you did as I requested but at the same time, you took your nasty ass back there and made the shit without gloves. You've been touching money, credit cards, and probably been digging in your ass and not one time have I seen you wash your hands. Not that it would matter if you did, you still touched the food I have to consume without gloves! Now give me my money back!"

"I need to see a receipt." The cashier smirked.

"You're going to need a surgeon to get my foot out your ass if you don't return my money!"

"Here's the receipt."

Horace walked up with the receipt in hand. He gave it to the cashier then stepped close to Koko. The manager approached the counter and whispered lowly to the cashier and she headed to the back of the restaurant.

"I'm sorry about that. I will definitely have a talk with her soon after handling your refund. I'll be giving you back the funds for the entire order and will make sure your meal is prepared properly. Again, I apologize for what transpired."

"I appreciate the fact you're willing to go the extra mile, but I'll just take the refund and be on my way," Koko said nice as she possibly could.

She knew how fast-food workers were when they were angry. Koko wasn't about to trust anyone in there to handle her food. She was always taught not to eat from an establishment where there was any type of altercation then allow them to prepare something she had to eat. There was no telling what would be done behind the scenes.

After receiving the refund, Koko and Horace walked out. She looked around to see what other restaurants were in the area. Instead of going to Taco Bell or Burger King, Koko went back to the truck settling for a bag of chips to go along with her lemonade. Horace stood away from the truck as he smoked. Koko took the time to scroll her social media business page to pass time. Reading some of the comments made her heart swell. Seeing all of the five-star reviews and positive comments made her smile. Koko saw Jackie's name and knew there was some bullshit behind it.

J Bryant one day ago

"Don't do business with this person. I ordered an African American Boss Baby cake and it looked like Trick Daddy in the face. When I reached out to Koko, she refused to give my money back and blocked me. This woman is a fraud! The photos are not real. She gets them all from google."

Koko laughed because Jackie of all people knew there wasn't anything fraudulent about her business. She set herself up by posting that mess because folks were dragging her in the comments. Koko started reading some of them and she smiled the entire time.

"A fraud where? I've ordered from this business several times and the young lady was professional from the start. One day I'm going to be able to experience on of her bigger pieces but I have to stack my coins. J Bryant, you sound like a hater. I highly recommend Koko Kakes & More."

"Isn't this your friend? Damn shame how the ones closest to you are the biggest haters."

"You mad, huh? Karma is going to spin the block on Koko's behalf. Your day is coming."

"Jackie, I know you in real life and I can't believe you would try to tarnish this woman's reputation like this. That ass whooping at the club wasn't enough, I see. Koko isn't for play play. LOL"

Koko shook her head while exiting out of the app. She wanted to delete Jackie's review but decided against it. Koko would allow the public to crucify and embarrass her for the day. Maybe it will humble her dumb ass. Horace sat in the passenger seat just as Koko laughed out loud.

"What's funny?"

"Go to my business page on the blue app," Koko replied as she started the car. "Find the comment Jackie left on there."

Horace read silently then yelled, "I know you fuckin' lying!" causing Koko to laugh some more. "I told you that bitch was jealous of you a long time ago. There's more to her that you don't know. Watch what I tell you. The rumble at the club was just the tip of the iceberg. You gon' have to bloody that hoe next time around."

"Not worth my time. I have too much to lose. Jackie doesn't have anything to lose. She's not shit without me and Cyrus. Life is going to beat the fuck out of her so I won't have to."

"That's true indeed. Jackie is going to try you again, Koko. Be ready." Horace paused. "I've never mentioned this, but I will now. I believe there's more to Jackie and Cyrus' relationship. I've seen how she looks at you whenever we were out together. Either she wants what you and Cyrus had or she already had it."

"Whatever rocks their boat. Neither one of them are my concern anymore." Koko yawned as she put the gear in drive.

"I'll take over the road so you can get some sleep. Switch places with me."

Koko didn't protest because she was tired as hell. The moment she sat in the passenger seat and her head hit the headrest; she was out like a light. Koko slept the rest of the way to Chicago until Horace shook her awake when they arrived at the venue. The drivers beat her there by forty-five minutes and the locomotive was stored and intact. Koko thanked them for their service and sent them on their way after giving instructions for her truck and keys. The guest of honor, Stephan McCormick greeted Koko as she entered, popping a peppermint in her mouth.

"Miss Simmons, thank you so much for bringing my vision to life. It's going to be the highlight of the night. Get ready because business is about to skyrocket for you after this, young lady."

"No, thank you for giving me a chance to show you, my talent. I really appreciate you for believing in me."

"You don't have to thank me. I put in the order and you put in the work. Producing exactly what I wanted. You did not disappoint. One thing I will do is look out for people that looked like me. Once I looked into your craft, I knew getting your name out into the mainstream was something that needed to be done. There's money out here for all of us. Doing whatever I can for a talented black man or woman is my daily mission."

"We need more people like you in this world, Mr. McCormick. Paying it forward is my mission as well. It's great to know someone who gave me a chance has a good heart. You will be the person I look up to from now on."

"No doubt. All you have to do is call and I'm there," Stephen said pulling a business card from his jacket pocket. "Go get some sleep and enjoy my city, Miss Simmons. It's a beautiful place in spite of the tragic stories the media spews."

Koko chuckled. "Please call me Kameeko or Koko. I'm very familiar with Chicago because it's my city too. Born and raised in the Grand Crossing area." Koko revealed. "I love my city but I can't stand the people who are bringing it down. I had to leave in order to enjoy life. Something has to give because our youth is suffering. That's a conversation for another day though. Enjoy the rest of your night and I'll see you tomorrow at the event."

Koko and Stephen hugged before parting ways. Horace waited in the truck patiently for his friend to finish conducting business. When Koko got back inside, he drove toward the hotel they would be staying. Following the directions to the W hotel, Horace pulled into the garage and found a spot to park. They got out to retrieve their luggage from the back before locking up and headed to the elevators. Horace looked around with a smile as he took in the elegance of the elevator. The doors opened to the lobby floor and he gasped loudly.

"Koko, this is an expensive hotel."

"It is but when a wealthy black man books the room in your name and foot the bill, go with the flow."

"Whewww chile, I wanna be like you when I grow up," Horace exclaimed. "Wait, we're sharing a room?"

"No, boo. I know how you get down. I don't want to be a witness to your sexual activities. You're on your own with that shit." Koko laughed.

"I respect your honesty. At least you are aware that I'd bring somebody's daddy back to satisfy me. It was part of your plan too. The way you and Mr. Money Man was smiling at each other, you may have plans in the making and don't even know it. I saw y'all through the window. I wouldn't blame you one bit either."

"Nope. Not going to happen. The motto *to get over a man is to get under another* is not my forte. I value my pussy, boo. I'm here for business and business only."

Koko stepped up to the counter and gave the concierge her name then retrieved the key cards. She listened as the woman explained all of the amenities that were available to them along with the room numbers. Horace was going into room 912, while Koko was taking the suite in 908. She didn't tell Horace there was a difference, but he probably wouldn't care because he was on vacation for free. Still, Koko was going to wait until he knocked so he could see for himself where her hard work had taken her.

Once the two stepped off the elevator on the ninth floor, Horace looked for his room while Koko stood in front of hers. They agreed to rest before meeting up for dinner. Inserting the key card into the slot, Koko entered the suite with a smile. It had been a while since she could lay back and relax without stress. She kicked her shoes off then prepared to shower. Koko prayed for a fun visit as she sat on the edge of the bed.

Chapter 6

"Kazimir, did you leave that white woman yet?" Pax asked. "I will not leave this earth while you're still being the slave master's son."

"She's Italian, paw-paw."

"Same difference. She ain't black," Pax retorted.

Pax's dementia was worsening by the day. Every day he said something racial about Kaz being with Nicolette. Pax didn't remember how his grandson ended up in the predicament he was in, or he just didn't want to remember. Kaz would never know and he didn't regret his decision. He sat listening because he knew Pax meant every word of what he said. Kaz wondered all the time how his grandpa got himself caught up with Santoro when he didn't like his kind.

"You do know she's using you to be the pappy to her Caucasian baby, right? I hope you got the DNA test done like I told you to before signing the birth certificate." Pax said cutting his eyes at Kaz. "The only thing a white woman wants from a black man is his money. When she doesn't get it, she's going to call the police saying you're beating on her."

"Paw-paw, how was your day?" Kaz asked changing the subject.

"My day was good. I went into the field and led the way into enemy territory in the tank. I protected the troops by shooting the opps dead. They were shooting back but I was well protected by some heavy artillery. We celebrated our victory in the mesh hall."

It amazed Kaz how Pax went from present to past in a blink of an eye. The stories he told were funny and very entertaining. Pax had been through some shit back in the day. His war stories were the best in Kaz's opinion.

"Are you ready for the next mission?" Kaz asked sitting back on the sofa.

"Oh, noooo. I retired. It's a good thing too because had I not, Barbara Jean wouldn't have bumped into me at the airport." Pax smiled as he thought about his wife. "Man, that woman was the true definition of a black queen. Barb stood five feet three inches, fat ass, big breasts, chocolate complexion, and an afro that would put any woman's hair to shame. Her voice alone almost brought me to my knees every time I heard it."

Pax looked around as if he anticipated someone to walk into the room at any moment. Kaz paid attention to him closely in case his grandpa made a sudden move. The question he asked next closed Kaz's throat completely.

"Did Barbara Jean come back from the grocery store? She's been gone quite some time now. I can taste the collard greens, smoked meat, honey cornbread, and yams."

Kaz pulled his phone from his pocket sending a text to his chef. He mentioned the foods Pax spoke of so it would be ready for dinner. The small delay gave Kaz time to get his thoughts together. He dreaded telling his grandpa about Barbara Jean's departure from life, but he did so on a daily basis.

"Paw-paw, Barbara Jean went home with the Lord. She's forever here in spirit."

"I know," Pax said as tears welled in his eyes. "She's waiting for me." He smiled. "We will be together again. Your mother told me to tell you she loves you, Kellan."

Pax's mind was running wild. It never made sense for Kaz to correct his grandpa once he referenced him as his father.

Playing along was easier because the information that followed was always lucrative. Kaz missed the days he and Pax would hang out fishing, shooting wild animals, and playing chess. He dreaded the day he would have to say goodbye to the only person left who meant anything to him.

"David came by the other day." Those words perked Kaz's ears up. "He stole more of my money, Kellan. I didn't raise that boy to steal from me. Raising the two of you wasn't an easy task, you know. It's the reason I worked my ass off to have my own business. So my son's wouldn't have to struggle in a world that was against them."

Pax looked away wiping at his eyes. "Kellan, I didn't approve of what you did in the streets, and still don't. But you are a grown man with your own family to look after. How you obtain your money is on you. Just take care of Kazimir. Promise to never have him selling that shit. The poison you are passing around the community. Make sure you leave him with a nice nest egg; he's going to need it with the life you're living. Plus, it will mean a lot to him knowing his father thought enough of him to make sure he would be good after you're gone. Those you think are friends are going to be the reason I bury you son."

At some point, Pax had that exact conversation with Kelo. Obviously, he didn't take heed to his father's warning. Kaz was sure his father knew how the game operated, and it was the reason he stayed behind the scenes of his street business. There was a high chance of ending up in prison or dead. Kelo didn't foresee the very man he deemed a brother putting a hit out on him. Kaz tried his best to learn from his father's mistakes. His right-hand man was a businessman like himself and he knew nothing about the side hustle that brought Kaz millions of dollars a year.

"Paw-paw, what is David into?" Kaz asked.

Pax's face lit up and he no longer appeared sad. Kaz would call him by the name only he used to address his grandpa to bring him back to the present. Even if it was for a short time. Pax sat quietly for more than five minutes before he shifted in the recliner he sat in.

"David is addicted to gambling. It started with one huge win that he has been chasing since. A smart person would understand the concept of gambling and the fact of it being a one in a thousand chance to hit big anytime soon after the first. Not David. He dug himself into a hole and I didn't realize how deep until it was too late. When he depleted his account and spent every dime of his salary; that's when he started in on my fortune."

Kaz knew the amount of money his uncle had taken from Pax; he just didn't know why. His grandfather bypassed that question for years. Until that moment. Hearing David used the money gambling pissed Kaz off. He had gotten St. Claire Candies back on its feet in just two years. David hadn't been around, and it was in his best interest to stay gone. Pax changed his will before he summoned Kaz home and he was officially Power of Attorney of his grandfather's estate. The bank had called Kaz when his uncle tried to withdraw money. He was denied because Kaz took him off all of the accounts and cancelled the cards in the process.

Pax was chilling with his eyes closed. Kaz wanted to suggest he go to his room but that would only make his grandpa regain his energy. He decided to go with his first mind and allow Pax to rest. Kaz wished every night his grandpa would agree to come live with him. He had suggested it on many occasions, but Pax always stated the same thing every time.

"I'm not staying under the same roof as that white woman. Plus, I have my own house. Getting it built from the ground just to move out is not going to happen. You can always come visit anytime you want, Kazimir."

Respecting his wishes, Kaz had been doing just that every day for the past couple years. He hired several home health aides to care for Pax. Seven days a week three aides rotated shifts to help Kaz out. The overnight aide arrived at eight and

89

didn't leave until eight. It was pretty easy money because all she was required to do was make sure Pax was in bed at night, showered, and fed in the morning. The aide who came on in the morning stayed for nine or ten hours until Kaz showed up. Thus far, there hadn't been any complaints.

Kaz made sure he had eyes on Pax every waking minute. He installed cameras throughout the house. Kaz prayed daily that he wouldn't have to kill someone for mistreating his grandfather. His phone vibrating on the table caught his attention. When he saw the name on the screen, Kaz wanted to decline the call. Instead, he answered it.

"Hello, Nicolette."

"Non rispondere al telefono come se fossi uno dei tuoi client, Kazimir."

Kaz didn't know any language other than English and Nicolette knew that. She talked to him in Italian whenever she was upset about something. The marriage he was in was not real in Kaz's eyes. It was for show and that was exactly how he portrayed it in private then barely in public. Nicolette on the other hand wanted to play wifey all year round. Kaz wasn't falling for the bullshit though. He didn't contribute a dime to the wedding. Santoro footed the bill down to the wedding rings. The only thing Kaz had done was signed on the dotted line. At times, he regretted doing that but for the sake of his grandfather, he went ahead with the foolery.

"I've told you time again to speak to me in a way I can understand. Leave that Italian shit for your family and friends." Kaz sighed.

"For the record, I said, don't answer the phone like I am one of your clients," she snapped.

"What is it?"

"Where are you? It's almost dinnertime and you are still not home. Aleesia is asking for you too."

"Every day you ask the same question, at the same time of day. When I'm doing something different, I won't hesitate to let you know. In all honesty, I really don't have to check in with you. It's not like you're my wife for real."

"You always say that and you know it's far from the truth! When you said I do at the alter before God, that made me Mrs. St. Claire. I'm tired of you downplaying this marriage. It's time we start living as husband and wife, Kazimir."

"I will continue reminding you of the arrangement your father forced me into. We will never be what normal people call being married. I did this shit for my grandfather but also for Alessia to have a daddy. I've held my end of the bargain by marrying you and I've also gone over and beyond for my daughter."

"Oh, now she's your daughter. If you can claim her as yours to me and others, why won't you sign the birth certificate?" Nicolette questioned Kaz further to keep the argument going. "Make it make sense because I'm not understanding."

Kaz didn't want to say what was on the tip of his tongue because he still had to sleep in the same house as her. When Nicolette became angry, she turned into a she-devil. The last thing Kaz wanted to do was get into a physical altercation with her because then, he would have to kill her father and brothers. Nicolette tried hard to push his buttons but he never took it there with her. Kaz learned how to walk away by going to his penthouse instead of battling with her. He tried his best not to leave the house because Alessia would cry for him sometimes and he wanted to be there when that happened.

"So, you not going to respond?"

"No, I'm not. We've been through this countless times and my response will not change. Soon as the caretaker gets here, I'll be on my way home. Until then, I need you to make sure you'll be ready for the black-tie event tomorrow."

"I'm not worried about no damn party!"

"Bye, Nicolette."

Kaz ended the call as he ran his hand down his face. He glanced over to check on Pax and was met with a blank stare. Seeing his grandpa sitting stoically without blinking scared Kaz. He jumped to his feet and rushed over to the recliner.

"Sit yo' ass down. I'm alright," Pax said before Kaz could check to see if he was breathing.

"Paw-paw, why were you dazed out like that?"

"I wasn't dazed, shit! I'm trying to figure out why you didn't tell that white woman how you really feel. The look on your face lets me know she talks to you like you're her son. Your black ass tiptoed around the truth instead of voicing the fact you don't love her pale ass. She's stressing you out, Kazimir. You better go out and get you some black coochie. I swear you will start smiling again. The blacker the berry, the sweeter the juice. You can't go wrong."

Kaz couldn't do nothing but laugh at Pax. He sounded like a young thug because his grandfather didn't allow that type of talk at his older age. Dementia had him walking through all the stages of his life.

"What you know about coochie?" Kaz asked, testing the waters.

"Boy, I'll slap the taste out your mouth! I'm not one of your little friends. Don't ever ask me no mess like that. What even possessed you to bring up a conversation like that to me?"

And just like that, Pax didn't recall initiating the conversation. Kaz was saved when the doorbell rang. He stood and made his way to open the door. The caretaker and the chef were standing in wait.

"Good evening," Kaz greeted. He stepped back, allowing them to come inside. He held his hand out to assist Marco, his chef, with the heated bags he carried.

Marco shook his head as he stepped over the threshold. "I can handle it, Mr. St. Claire. Thank you though."

Kaz locked the door before turning to check on Pax. He was talking with Kelly as she took his vitals. He had the biggest smile on his face as Kelly did everything she was paid to do. Pax liked her out of all the caretakers, and he never gave her any problems. Kaz wished she could be his live-in caretaker, but he was quite sure she had a life outside of her job.

"Mr. St. Claire, I want to give you a heads up. I will have to draw blood to take to your doctor. We will do it in the morning before breakfast, okay?"

"You know I don't like needles. All that poking and probing to still get it wrong. Tell the doctor I refused to give it to you. What is he going to do, lock me up?" Pax fussed.

"I know you did not put me in the category of those other folks who comes here to help you. Do you remember who I am? I'm Kelly. You don't even flinch when I draw your blood. There's always a smile on your handsome face when I'm around."

"Ohhh, Brown Suga! I didn't recognize you at first. Stop getting fresh with me. I'm too old to make you my wife but my grandson is available. Ain't that right, Kazimir?"

Kelly blushed because she did have somewhat of a crush on Kaz. She kept her feelings under wraps because he was married. Kelly didn't believe in messing around with something that didn't belong to her. Pax always talked about his grandson and constantly tried to convince her to shoot her shot. Kelly laughed it off every time. So, that day, she concentrated on her client and not the words being said around her.

"Paw-paw, you know I'm not available. Kelly don't listen to this man sitting here," Kaz chortled. "Thank you for all you do for him. I know I've done so many times over, but I want to really let you know how much I appreciate how you handle Mr. Hardhead."

"Watch yourself, son. Not too much on me, okay?" Pax shot back. "You better get you a beautiful black queen that's going to hold you down just like Barbara Jean does for me."

Kaz shook his head at his grandfather because he was going to stand on what he said.

"You are very welcome, Mr. Kazimir. I take pride in the career I've chosen. My passion for caring is real. I went to school for nursing while taking care of people. The moment I stepped into the hospital setting; I knew I would fail. The environment was not sitting right with my spirit. The way the doctors spoke to and treated the nurses wasn't for me because I will never allow anyone to bully or belittle me. Not to mention, the care of the patients wasn't a priority. Especially, people of color. So, I made a choice and stayed in the profession I loved. And that was care taking. The only difference now is, I can administer medications, help with picc lines, IVs, catheters, and etcetera. I take pride in what I do and goes above and beyond for the ones I come to love."

Hearing Kelly talk about how much she loved what she did in life, had both Kaz and Pax's attention. She had a loving heart, and her story was satisfying to listen to. Pax looked over at Kaz and he already knew what he had to do.

Marco stood in the entryway of the kitchen. "Dinner is ready," he announced.

Kaz assisted Pax to his feet then led him to the dining room. Kelly stayed behind as she sat on the sofa. He was puzzled as to why she was not coming to join them. It would be rude to eat in her presence and she was in the living room alone. That wasn't how the St. Claire family operated.

"Hey, Kelly, come join us for dinner."

"Yes, you are family, Brown Suga. Get in here and get some of this good food," Pax said over his shoulder.

Kelly walked in and sat down across from Kaz. Marco placed several dishes on the table, and it was everything Kaz asked him to cook as well as jerk chicken, and macaroni and cheese. The food smelled good, and Kelly's mouth watered. She hadn't had a meal like grandmas in a very long time. She was used to ordering food to be delivered because she was too tired to cook after the long hours of working. Kelly had three clients she helped care for, but Mr. St. Claire was her favorite. She always wished she could make life work by having one client. The economy made it very impossible for people nowadays.

Kelly worked hard to provide for herself. Making good money had nothing on the economy because she was still only making ends meet. She didn't have time to have fun and smile outside of making her clients happy. Kelly slept on her off days, only going out for special occasions. She was due for a vacation but didn't want to put Mr. St. Caire in the hands of another longer than needed. The older man was a ray of sunshine when he was feeling good. Times could be hard for him when his days were a bit lower. No matter the day, Kelly was always there to uplift him and get him back on track.

"What are you over there thinking about?" Kazimir asked as he filled his plate.

"Nothing much. Thank you, guys, for including me." She sighed. "I really appreciate it. I haven't had a meal like this in years."

"Why is that?" Kaz inquired.

She reached out to get some food and spooned small portions on her plate. Kelly didn't want to appear greedy, so she kept things light. The mac and cheese were creamy with a nice crust on top. She couldn't wait to see if it tasted good as it looked.

"Girl, put some food on that plate," Pax said glaring at her the same way her granny used to. "You need some meat on them bones. There's more than enough for you to eat much as you like. Ain't no shame when you're in my house."

Kelly laughed and dug in, serving herself larger portions. When she finally placed everything she wanted on her plate, Pax grabbed her left hand and Kaz reached for the other. She was confused at first until she realized what they were doing. Kelly hadn't prayed since her grandmother passed away. When Pax started saying grace over the food, tears fell from her eyes. He recited the Psalm Prayer which her grandma always recited during dinner.

"The eyes of all look to you, O Lord, and you give them their food at the proper time. You open your hand and satisfy the desire of everything living. Thank you for the meal. Amen."

Kelly opened her eyes and once again, Kazimir and Pax were staring at her. She held her head down as she discretely wiped at the tears. Bringing down the vibe at the table was something Kelly didn't want to do. She waited for the questions because she knew they were coming.

"Is everything alright?" Kazimir asked with concern.

"Yeah, I'm fine. My granny passed away and the prayer just reminded me of her. That's all."

"I'm sorry to hear that. My condolences."

"It's been two years but still feels like yesterday. I've been getting through the best I can. It has been rough but I keep a smile on my face for the sake of my clients. Without them, I would be a nervous wreck."

They sat quietly eating before another word was spoken. Just as Kelly expected, the food was topnotch. She was moaning lowly with every bite.

"Brown Suga, you over there being nasty with those greens, I see," Pax joked. "I know how you feel because they shole is good."

Kelly used a napkin to wipe her mouth while trying to hide the fact she was blushing. "They are very delicious."

"Kelly, let me ask you something," Kazimir said clearing his throat. She nodded as she waited patiently for whatever he wanted to know. "How many clients do you have?"

"I have three. Mr. St. Claire is the only one I take care of overnight. When I leave here, I go to another client for a few hours. The third client I only work with a couple days out of the week, but those two days are the ones I work round the clock."

Kazimir put his fork down then wiped his mouth and hands on a napkin. He needed to know why Kelly was working the way she was. To him, it didn't sound as if she had a social life at all. From what he gathered, she was kind of in the world alone since her grandmother's passing, she was working instead of living life and it was probably because she couldn't afford to take time off. Kelly was overworked to say the least. Kazimir was always down to help anyway he could. Thanks to his good friend Stephan McCormick, Kazimir always looked for the good in his people.

"Kelly, I have a proposition for you." He paused. "How about I cut the hours you work here…"

"I can't afford for you to do that. The twelve hours I'm here brings in the bulk of my salary." She said interjecting immediately.

"Hear me out. What I meant was, how about you work with my grandfather full-time, and I will double your salary. On top of that, you can move here and become his live-in caretaker. All expenses included. If you don't have transportation, one will be appointed to you. That way, you can save money and get out during the day to enjoy what you like to do."

Thinking about what he had offered, Kazimir said the right things but didn't consider if any of it aligned with her living situation. "One more thing. Are you married, involved, or have any children?"

Kelly chuckled. "Fine time to ask, but no. I've been single for the past two years and I'm not financially stable to take care of another human right now. Your offer is very tempting, but I will feel bad leaving my other clients behind."

"I'm sure the agency can find someone just as good as you to cover those patients. Maybe you can even recommend someone you trust."

"Brown Suga, you better jump on this opportunity. The man is trying to help you financially and maybe, just maybe, you can make him fall in love with you so he can get away from that noncolored gal."

"Paw-paw! Cut it out," Kazimir chastised him. "That is not my intentions at all, Kelly. I just want to make sure you are able to save and get your finances together. You don't have to give me an answer at this moment. You can tell me what you decide when the time is right for you."

"Thank you. I promise to let you know my decision soon. In case you want to find another candidate if I turn the offer down."

Kazimir tilted his head to the side. "Kelly, this is an exclusive deal for you. There will be no other person I trust to do the job I'm laying at your feet. So, think about it, okay?"

Kazimir stood picking up his plate. He walked to the kitchen and scrapped the food into the trash then proceeded to wash the dishes. Strolling back to the table he kissed Pax on top of his head hugging him tightly.

"I'm going to get out of here, paw-paw. I want to get home to see Alessia before she goes to sleep. I'll see you early tomorrow just to check in on you."

"Okay. Do me a favor. Don't give that white woman no dingaling."

"Bye, man." Kazimir laughed as he walked out of the kitchen. "Goodnight, Kelly. Think about what I said."

Kazimir didn't wait for her response. He left the house and jumped in his car. He cranked the ignition and turned the volume up on his system. Nipsey's *Hustle and Motivate* led him to his destination.

***

Soon as Kaz pulled into the gate surrounding his home, the phone rang. He knew it had nothing to do with St. Claire Candies because it was damn near eight o'clock at night. He looked down and saw Lowkey's name on the stereo display. Taking a deep breath, Kaz answered. "Yo!"

"Nigga, we got a problem. The trap in the Willard-Hay hood."

"Correction, *you* got a muthafuckin' problem. I'm not out in the streets. That's why I put you in charge. Every time something happens you calling me to see what needs to be done. If you can't handle yo' position, say that shit. It would be nothing for me to get another nigga out there to take over!"

"Man, Kaz, you always hollerin' about how you not hands-on with this shit. You don't have a problem collecting the bread though."

Lowkey must've forgotten who the fuck runs the entire Midwest. The nigga was real loose at the lips since his muthafuckin' club was bringing in hell of money. What he failed to realize was Kaz was the type of nigga that would snatch that shit from under his ass. That's not the type of nigga he was but Lowkey was letting the suits and intellectual speech cloud his judgement on how to talk to the man in charge.

Kaz and Kazimir were two different muthafuckas. Kazimir the businessman was professional at all times. He wore designer suits, crisp button-down shirts, ties, and diamond cufflinks. He was soft spoken, very intelligent, and stayed in a business mindset. Kaz on the other hand didn't give a fuck. He didn't wear suits, but he dressed down like a street nigga with fitted caps pulled low over his eyes. Kaz never roamed the streets without heat on his hip. When Kaz pushed Kazimir out the way, blood was about to be shed. Nine times out of ten, some stupid muthafucka was playing with his money. In Lowkey's case, he was testing Kaz's manhood.

"You muthfuckin' right I'm coming for mine. Don't leave out the fact that I pay yo' ass a substantial amount of that shit and you still can't handle shit on yo' own. Make that shit make sense, nigga. What the fuck I'm paying you for?"

"I can handle this. You didn't even let me tell you what the problem is," Lowkey gritted.

"And I'm still not because I don't want to hear that shit! You the muthafuckin' boss of them niggas! Take care of whatever it is. I'll hit yo' line day after tomorrow and it better be handled, or your problem will be minor compared to the problem yo' ass will face if I have to pull up."

Kaz banged on Lowkey's ass tossing the phone into the passenger seat. He had to calm down before going into the home because neither Nicolette or Alessia ever seen him in the mode he was in. Kaz was so mad because his business in Minnesota was his worse headache. Anytime something went down, he was being called. Any other state took care of business and contacted him after the fact. Not those niggas in the Twin Cities. Kaz didn't want to head out to Minneapolis, but at that point, he may not have a choice. Lowkey was showing his weakness and that shit was unacceptable. Picking his phone up, Kaz shot Steelo a text.

Kaz: I'm going to need you to ride out with me to Minnesota in a few days. I'll fill you in later.

Finally ready to go inside his home, Kaz exited his vehicle and walked slowly up the steps. Had it not been for Alessia he would've gone to the city and slept at the penthouse he owned downtown in the Water Tower Place. Entering the code into the keypad, Kaz pushed the door open and was greeted by an angry Nicolette. At the same time, his phone notification sounded. He looked at it and saw Steelo had responded.

Steelo: Bet. Just keep me posted. I'm down for whatever.

Kaz put the device into his pocket then looked up at Nicolette.

"We need to talk," she said folding her arms over her chest.

"About?"

Kaz walked by her making sure to toe his shoes off at the door. He made his way to the sitting room and sat on the sofa. Nicolette followed without a word then stood next to him. Kaz could feel her staring a hole into the side of his head.

"Have a seat. I think we can communicate better if we're both sitting. Get rid of the attitude while you're it at too, Nicolette."

She huffed as she walked around the coffee table then plopped on the love seat across from him. The way Nicolette was carrying on, she reminded him of Alessia when she couldn't get her way and she was two years old. It was time for Kaz to speak direct and point blank on their *marriage*. Nicolette walked into the situation just as blind as he had. He couldn't understand the confusion.

"I know what this is about," Kaz said leaning forward with his elbows resting on his knees. "We have been playing this game of pretend for two years. It's nothing new."

"How after so long haven't you tried to even sleep with me?" Nicolette asked. "Most of the time we don't sleep in the same bed. When we do, you don't even touch me."

"This has never been a physical thing for me," he stated.

"This? It's a marriage, Kazimir," she said before he could finish his thought.

"We were forced into this, Nicolette. I didn't meet you one day and my heart skipped a beat. Getting to know each other wasn't an option either. Your father threatened my grandfather and I'm still on his ass about that shit," Kaz snapped. Closing his eyes, Kaz took a deep breath because he didn't want to take his anger out on Nicolette. It wasn't her fault. It did put her in an awkward position though. Santoro was not allowed anywhere near his property. In order for him to see Nicolette and Alessia, they had to meet elsewhere.

"Look, I only agreed to go through with this because my family was at risk. I never promised to love you. Don't get it twisted, I respect you as Alessia's mother. That's it, that's all.

How many times have I told you to go out, have fun, and live your life? In case you didn't understand, that also meant find someone to give you the sexual gratification you crave."

"I don't want to find anyone else! I have a whole husband. You should be the one satisfying me sexually. It's what a husband is supposed to do."

"Nicolette, that's not how this works. It would be easy for me to ram my dick in and out of you but it wouldn't do anything but bring more harm than good into this household. I'm not willing to jeopardize my peace more than I've already done by marrying you."

"It doesn't matter how we came about, Kazimir! You are my husband! If you're not having sex with me, who are you having sex with?"

Kaz was never one to lie and he had no plans of starting in that moment. Hurting Nicolette's feelings was far from his intent, but it had to be done. Giving her hope wasn't in his game plan either. He needed her to understand their union was a business deal. There was no other way around what he was about to say.

"Actually, it doesn't matter who I'm sleeping with. That's none of your concern. I'm gon' keep it solid with you though, I have my share of women I get with so I'm not tempted to come in this muthafucka and slut yo' ass out. In reality, Nicolette, I'm saving you from the effects my dick would have on you. No, I'm not bragging. Just stating facts."

"I can't believe you said that to me!" she cried.

"What do you want me to do, lie? I'm not gon' do that to you. Blowing smoke up yo' ass is not my style. Your daddy can continue to tell you I'm the man for you. I won't hop on that train. If anything, I'm going to keep it a buck with you. Sexually, I'm good in that department. Getting with women isn't hard for a man of my stature."

"Who is she?" Nicolette exclaimed.

"Who is who?" Kaz asked confused.

"The woman you're treating me like shit for!"

"Would you lower your voice, Nicolette?" he asked nicely. "You have done enough yelling and it's uncalled for. Alessia is upstairs sleeping. You're worrying about a woman that doesn't exist. I don't have anyone special in my life. The women I deal with always leave my presence without expectations of being with me. When they start showing they want more, that's the end because it's not what I'm looking for," Kaz explained more than he should have but it was necessary.

"You have to think about how your actions could affect Alessia. She doesn't need to see you and I constantly at each other's throats. And she damn sure doesn't need to see you with different women."

"Alessia would never see me with random women. None of them knows anything about me other than how many times my dick can touch the fleshy ball in the back of their throats. So, they damn sure won't be meeting her."

"My baby needs both her mama and daddy to be all-in when raising her!"

"Then go find her muthafuckin' daddy," Kaz said without thought.

"You are her daddy!"

"Nah, and let's address this shit while we're on the subject. There's a difference between a daddy and a father. By default, I'm her father. Alessia will forever be able to depend on me to be there for her. What I will not accept is you trying to use her to pressure me to love you. She will always be my daughter and I won't be signing papers to prove it. The only reason I would sign the birth certificate is if you were on your deathbed. Nothing matters in this shit except her."

"Daddy! Daddy! Daddy!"

On cue, Alessia small cries bellowed from one of the many monitors Kaz had installed around his home so she could be heard at all times. Kaz stood to his feet and headed for the stairs. Nicolette glared at her husband's back. The

103

urge to stab him in it became stronger with every step he took. As the seconds ticked, her dislike for Kazimir grew tremendously. Nicolette refused to allow him to dismiss her as if he didn't vow to love and cherish her. What he took lightly was the fact he agreed to do those things 'til death.

Chapter 7

"Fuck, Jack!"

With her ass spread, face buried in a pillow, and hands gripping the sheets, Jackie was enjoying the back shots that were being delivered to her yoni. The moans escaped her lips bouncing off the hotel walls. Jackie waited a long time for the treatment she was receiving. Sex with the sneaky link was always damn good. It was something about getting dick that belong to somebody else. Jackie didn't care what took place after she left the nigga. Long as she got her nut, anything after that wasn't her concern.

"Damn, you wettin' this muthafucka up! Throw that ass back, bae."

Jackie hated when he talked as if she was his bitch. It was part of the reason she stayed away so long because his feelings were always laid out on the table when they were doing the sexual tango. Love wasn't part of the equation. Jackie wasn't trying to be bae, boo, baby, none of that to these niggas. If he could cheat on his girl with her, his ass could do the same to her if given the chance. Being in a relationship was something Jackie was afraid of because she cheated back. A dude would be looking for her in the daytime with a flashlight after he had wronged her.

Watching Koko be dumb for Cyrus was a pitiful sight. Jackie pitied her former friend in the beginning. After basically telling her what she needed to do, Koko still stayed while he continued to do her wrong. At that point, Jackie didn't feel bad for her because if she liked it, Jackie loved it.

Jackie's head was yanked back, causing her to cum hard. She opened her eyes in time to dodge the kiss dude tried to plant on her lips. She wasn't having it. There was nothing wrong with the act they performed together but kissing was where she drew the line. He may have forgotten the rules, but Jackie hadn't.

"You fuckin' up the vibe, Jackie," he said stroking harder hitting her spot repeatedly.

"That's right; make this pussy cry! Fuck me harder!" Jackie screamed out. "Yup, just like that."

"This my pussy, Jack. You know I love you, right?"

"Concentrate on making me cum, nigga. You don't love me. You love my doggy style."

Her sarcasm got her the best orgasm she'd had in months. Talking shit was her way to keep love making out of the mix. Fucking was all she wanted out of the deal. The monetary reward was extra on his part. It was the same routine every time the two hooked up.

"Deeper," she moaned. "Yes! Yes! I'm cummin'!"

When he inserted his thumb in her ass, it was over for both of them. Jackie's walls gripped his muscle tightly causing him to shoot every drop of his semen into the condom he wore. Her creamy juices coated his shaft bricking him up again. She had somewhere to be and going for round two was out of the question.

"Nope. Control your penis, sir. I have to go."

"Why you always do that bullshit, Jack? I put off the rest of my day for this."

"I don't know why you would do that. We have never laid up afterward. We're not about to start that shit now. I'm quite sure you can find something to do with the remainder of your day. It just won't be in this room fuckin' me."

The ringing of his phone was the thing Jackie needed to make her grand escape. Her plan was to shower then head to her destination. It wasn't going to happen that way because she couldn't be in the presence of anybody smelling like ass, dick, and pussy. So, her next stop would be to her house to take care of her hygiene. Stepping into her shoes, Jackie looked up as dude mugged the fuck out of her as he listened to whatever was being said on his line. She almost laughed out loud and she knew he was pissed by the way his jawline clenched. He couldn't say anything because he wouldn't want to expose what he did privately to whomever was on the other end of the call. Jackie blew a kiss toward him before walking out of the door.

Soon as she was comfortably in her car, she heard the text alert sound from her phone. She already knew who it was so she didn't bother checking it. Jackie drove through the streets as she jammed to Xscape's *My Little Secret* with a smile. She sang that song with her chest and had the nerve to replay it for good measures. It took twenty minutes to pull into the driveway of her townhome. She glanced at the clock on the dash and smacked her lips because she was behind schedule and didn't want to miss the opportunity to speak with Koko before she left her place of business.

Rushing in the house to take care of her hygiene, Jackie thought about the reason she wanted to make amends with the woman she grew to love. It was wrong for her to leave Koko in the dark about Cyrus' infidelities and the fact he had a baby. Jackie was put in the middle by being the best friend and the long-time sister-friend to Cyrus so she opted to keep her mouth shut. She didn't want to choose sides. But she should've been a woman first and put a buzz in Koko's ear all the same. Instead, she just kept telling her Cyrus wasn't shit and she needed to leave him alone.

What Jackie wanted to do was apologize for what she said in the bathroom of the club. It had been over a month, and she stalled every time the thought entered her mind to visit Koko. The way she whooped her ass, Jackie gave her time to calm down. Koko had every right to be mad at her for the words she heard. Jackie didn't think she would follow her to the bathroom. Sheree was smart to run her ass out of the confined space but dumb to hit Koko while her back was turned. She got the ass end of the stick and was going to get the full Monty when Koko caught up with her again.

Jackie dropped the clothes she took off and threw them in the hamper. She took a ten minute shower, dressed, and was back out the door in record time. Nervousness took over her body as she drove to Burnsville. She had practiced the words she wanted to say but at the moment they scrambled together in her brain. When she finally pulled in front of the building of Koko Kakes & More, the lights were off and there was a note on the inside of the glass door. She got out to read what it said.

Sorry for the inconvenience
Koko Kakes & More will be closed until next week. For any questions, please send an inquiry to my email address below. If you want to submit an order, head on over to Koko Kakes & More's website and complete the order form. Understand there will be delays until I return to the city. I'll be sure to contact you to follow up. Thank you and have a wonderful weekend.
Kameeko

Pulling her phone from her purse, Jackie hit Cyrus' name in the contacts list and walked back to her car as she waited for him to answer. When he didn't pick up, Jackie called him right back because she needed to know where Koko was. She knew how to manipulate the woman she spent countless days and nights with whenever she was in her feelings about her relationship. That was the time she could get any amount of money from her, and she was trying to get to that bread.

"I'm busy, Jackie. What's up?" Cyrus asked soon as the call connected.

"I just came to Koko's studio and she's not here. Do you know where she is?" She could hear him shuffling around but he didn't answer her question. "Cyrus—"

"Man, why are you pullin' up on her? You know she don't fuck with you no mo', Jackie. Leave that shit alone. And you about to be messy where she gets a bag. That's fucked up for real."

"I'm not on bullshit. I came to apologize to her. I miss my friend. How can I be wrong for that?" Jackie quizzed.

"It's not wrong if you are sincere with your reasons for wanting to apologize. We both know you don't give a fuck about her. Leave her alone. To answer your question, I don't know where she is. As you know, Koko isn't fuckin' with my ass either. The same way you lost her for not keeping shit real, I lost her by lying. I got the brute of the hit. But anyway, I gotta go. I'll holla at you later."

Cyrus ended the call before Jackie could say anything else. She put the car in reverse and backed out of the parking space. Her stomach growled and she needed to get something to eat while she was out. She had worked up an appetite with her sneaky link. Captain Hooks was calling out to her, and she could taste the catfish and fries with lots of lemon pepper the more she thought about it.

Jackie parked outside the restaurant and thought about where Koko could've gone as she got out of her vehicle. Anytime she had an event, Jackie was always there along with Horace sweet ass. There was something about him that Jackie didn't like. Maybe it was the fact he could see how fake she was. After ordering her food, Jackie waited patiently. She decided to order something for her mother because she was going to her house to check on her. Jackie wasn't ready to go home yet.

The door opened and she spotted Sheree's brother Jojo with his fine ass. He glanced around the restaurant as if he was scoping out the place. His eyes landed on Jackie with a smirk. Her lady parts started tingling erratically. One would think she would be satisfied from her encounter earlier but Jackie stayed ready to open her legs. She loved having sex that much.

"Sup, Jackie?"

"Hey, Jojo."

"You good? Need anything?" he asked licking his lips.

"Number 98!" The cashier called out her number, interrupting the shit that was bound to fall from Jackie's mouth.

She shook her head as she grabbed her food and left. Opening the door to her vehicle, Jackie lifted her leg to get inside when Jojo partially stepped out of the door.

"Aye, Jackie, you gon' stop playing hard to get one of these days. I know the only reason you ain't trying to let a nigga taste your sweetness is because you don't want to betray your boy, Cyrus. Don't let your loyalty to that nigga make you miss out on what could be the best thing to happen in your life."

"Bye, Jojo. I don't fuck with any of my homegirls' brothers. That shit fucks up friendships. Especially when our time is up. I only do hit and runs." She smirked. "Be easy though."

Jackie smiled hard as she sat behind the wheel, leaving Jojo standing where he stood. She used the lie about not fucking with her friends brothers because he didn't have enough money for her. Jojo, his brother and cousins been trying to get on Cyrus' payroll since they found out Sheree was fuckin' around with him. All of them niggas barely had a dollar to their name. Jojo had his own place and a whip, but he didn't hold the status Jackie needed in a man.

As she drove to her mother's home, she picked up her phone and dialed Koko's number. Jackie hoped she hadn't blocked her. The ringing of the phone told her that wasn't the case. It continued to ring through the speakers, and she just knew the call was going to voicemail when Koko answered with so much malice in her voice.

"Jacqueline Denise Bryant, why the fuck are you calling my phone?"

Koko was getting ready for the event that may change the dynamics of her career and this measly bitch was calling her phone bringing a dark cloud to ruin her mood. There wouldn't be any pleasantries because in her mind, Jackie didn't exist to her. She was right up shit creek with her homeboy. Koko would entertain her for maybe three minutes before she deleted and blocked her number so she couldn't reach out to her ever again.

"Damn, it's like that?"

"What do you mean? Jackie, you act like you weren't the same bitch talking down on me with a nothing ass hoe. Get the fuck outta here with that bullshit, man. You chose the side you're riding with. Stay yo' ass right over there. I was the realest muthafucka in your corner. You didn't want for shit when you were standing ten toes down beside me. Let me rephase that. I was standing ten toes down because obviously, some of your limbs didn't work when it was time for you to stand with me."

"Koko, I'm—"

"Yup. You're one sorry son of a bitch," Koko said, cutting her off. "I hope Cyrus' baby mama can hold you down the way I did because I know you're only trying to apologize because you want something. That shit won't work this time around. See, I been peeped how you moved. I bet you thought you had one of those gullible, naïve bitches as your friend. Nope. I helped you because I got it like that to do so. I know to only dish out what I can afford and not look for it back in return." Koko was on a roll and wasn't going to take a breath to allow her former friend to get a word in.

"For years you played in my face and I overlooked the shit. You were always throwing shots at me. Your jealousy was always front and center. Somebody else had to point that part out to me. I soaked it all in because I knew the day would come for me to beat yo' ass. My mission was accomplished and now it's time to put an end to this cat and mouse game of who my friends are. Long as I got me and God, I don't need another to walk beside me in all my glory. The things I did for you, Jackie, will come back to me ten times fold. My next good deed will go toward helping a homeless person because the people I thought I knew ain't shit! The next time you think about contacting me, don't!" Koko hung up on her.

Jackie was stunned because she was read like a book. To be honest, her feelings were hurt for a split second until Koko said she was jealous of her. There was never a day she was ever jealous of Koko. Did she wish she was in her position? Yes, because she had her shit together and Jackie didn't. Jackie could admit staying around to benefit from Koko's accomplishments. When they were shopping, she never had to reach in her pocket to pay for anything. So, hell yeah, she milked that cow for all it was worth.

Jackie cruised the rest of the way to her mother's house while boppin' to GloRilla's *Finesse*. The lyrics took her mind off the lack of conversation she'd just had with Koko. At that point, Jackie wanted to sit down and enjoy her food while chopping it up with her mama. When she pulled up on the block, the hood niggas were out in droves. Stella, Jackie's mom still lived in the same house she grew up in. When she parked in front of the house, all heads turned in her direction.

The car she was driving was one of the gifts Cyrus had purchased for her birthday a few months prior. Jackie even lied, telling Koko one of her sponsors bought it because she didn't want to reveal the fact she could get whatever she wanted from him. It wouldn't look good on his part that he was buying gifts like cars when he hadn't moved Koko out of the apartment she was living in. The shit would've caused all kinds of problems in their relationship. But Jackie didn't care how Koko felt after that day.

The niggas waited with mugs on their faces to see who was about to get out of the fully loaded 2024 Chevrolet

Traverse with the dark tint. It may not have been much to a lot of people, but it meant a lot to her because she would've never been able to get a vehicle on her own. So, she was grateful for what she was given. Even though she wished Cyrus had listened to what her dream car actually was. Then again, he probably did and wasn't buying the Benz she spoke so highly of without any means of buying it herself. Stepping out the car, Jackie revealed herself.

"Dammit, Jackie! Next time let the window down so a muthafucka can see that it's you. I was three seconds from riddling that bitch with some hot shit," a dude named John John said.

"You wasn't about to do shit. My mama would be out here returning the favor if you had."

Jackie slammed the door and stalked up the walkway. She turned briefly to lock up her vehicle and John John had something smart to say. He was always a thorn in her ass.

"Aye, Jackie, who bought you that whip? Yo' nigga Cyrus?"

"Stop playing with me John. Cyrus ain't my nigga. He is my forever friend. My brother."

"We all know you ain't crossing that line because Koko would tap that ass."

"Koko won't tap shit. Stop playing on my top."

"That's not what I heard. Was there piss on the floor in that bathroom?"

Everybody within earshot started laughing. Jackie was embarrassed to know people knew about the fight she had with Koko. The revelation pissed her off that she was the butt of all jokes in the hood. It only made Jackie want a round two to redeem herself. She couldn't allow one fight to determine she couldn't handle Koko. Flipping John John off, she hurried into her mother's house while vaguely hearing John John and his friends continue to talk about her. Jackie slammed the door, locking it behind her.

"Why the hell you slamming my door like that, Jackie?" Stella walked out of the kitchen wiping her hands on a dish rag.

"I brought you some catfish and chicken gizzards from Captain Hooks."

"Thank you, but what's your problem, Jackie?"

"Nothing. John John is out there being his same annoying self." she shrugged.

"Jaqueline, you know got damn well I'm not talking about John John. What the hell did you do to Kameeko?"

Hearing her mother speak on Koko shocked Jackie. She hadn't told her about what happened between them and never had any intention to do so. For Stella to have any recollection of the beef came as a surprise. It was barely a time Jackie had gone to her mother's house and Koko wasn't stepping in behind her. Stella looked at Koko as her second child. Especially since she didn't have the love from her own mother, Stella made sure to always provide love as a stand-in mother figure.

"I didn't do anything to her. Why are you coming at me like she's God's gift or something? You should've been asking why she put her hands on me!"

"Lil girl, if you raise your voice at me and in my house again, I'll slap the fuck out of you. Have you lost your mind?"

"No, but she has. You didn't even ask me what happened. I guess whatever Koko said is law," Jackie snapped.

"I've heard her side; now tell me yours."

Stella grabbed the bag with the food inside and took a seat at the table. Jackie stood watching her mama eat while thinking about how much she wanted to reveal. The silence was getting the best of her so she sat in the chair across from her mother and said fuck it to herself. She had never lied to her as an adult so she may as well just get it over with.

"You ready to talk?"

"Me and Koko have been friends since the first couple months she moved here. You know this. Fast forward. Cyrus has been fucking up… I'm sorry," she said apologizing for cursing. "He has been messing up their whole relationship. I've told Koko time again she needed to move on from Cyrus. I couldn't make her leave if that wasn't what she wanted to do."

"Tell me this, Jackie. Why didn't you as a friend flat out tell her what Cyrus was doing?"

"Cyrus has been my friend longer than Koko. What do you mean why didn't I tell her? He is my friend for life."

"And you called Koko your sister!" Stella yelled. "A nigga come and go, but a friendship is forever. Everything that woman has done for you should have earned one hundred percent of your loyalty. I don't give a damn how long you've been friends with Cyrus, Koko should've been your focal point. You sat back watching her get cheated on while smiling in her face. You were wrong, Jackie!"

"I'm wrong? How? Koko is a grown ass woman. She saw Cyrus with other women with her own eyes, but I'm wrong. She knew what was going on without me saying anything about the matter. The only thing I will admit to being wrong about is not exposing the baby he had on her."

"A baby! How old is this baby, Jackie?"

"Cj is a year old. Koko didn't even tell me she knew about the baby."

"Hell, she was waiting for you to tell her. As close as you are with Cyrus, she already had a feeling you were aware of it. I knew something was going on because Koko hasn't been over to see me in several months. That's unusual when she used to come by a couple days a week just to bring me something sweet." Stella shook her head in disbelief. "Tell me about the fight. How did that transpire?"

"She had diarrhea of the mouth, huh?" Jackie chuckled. "We were at the club and I noticed Sheree, Cyrus' baby mama, kissing another dude. When she went to the bathroom, I followed after telling Koko where I was going. I didn't expect her to follow me. She heard me saying some shit to Sheree and came in swinging."

"What did you say to piss her off though. I'm not understanding."

"I downplayed her position in Cyrus' life. I basically told Sheree she was winning because Cyrus didn't do half the shit for Koko that he did for her. Koko heard me, and got mad."

Stella took a few bites of fish and sat back. She stared at her daughter raging inside. In her mind, Jackie fucked over the only true friend she had in her corner.

"Answer me this. Are you fuckin' Cyrus?"

"Ma! Why would you ask me something like that? Cyrus is like a brother to me and I don't even look at him in that way. You're reaching and I don't like it. You are on the Koko train going against me. Your daughter!"

Jackie got up and snatching her food off the table. She was done with the accusations from her mother. Leaving was the best thing for her to do before she said something disrespectful.

"Don't run. Let's talk about this. Your defensiveness is telling me all I need to know. You're denying it, but I feel you are lying."

"I'm not lying! Fuckin' Cyrus is the last thing I'm doing. He is with Sheree when he's not with Koko. When the hell would I have time to sleep with him?" Jackie asked shaking her head. "You can believe whatever your narrative is; I don't have to stand here listening to it."

"Stop calling Koko's phone. She called asking me to have a talk with you. Koko doesn't want anything else to do with you. She has so much going on in her life and don't need the bullshit interfering with her growth. Stay away from her, Jackie. Lock the door on your way out. I love you."

Jackie walked out of her mother's home angry. She had never done that in her life because life was short, and you never know if something drastic would happen. Saying I love you was very important in their household. Jackie couldn't fix her mouth to say it back that day. She felt her mother turned against her but in reality, Jackie was wrong as two left feet.

She jumped in her vehicle and pulled away after tossing her food in the passenger seat. Her phone rang and she saw her mother calling. Jackie ignored the call then powered off her device. She'd had enough of the bullshit for one day and was over it. Instead, she turned the volume up on the radio as she headed home.

Chapter 8

Koko looked in the mirror as she admired the dress she chose to wear for the event. The top was a bodice design with small rimstones, and it showcased her stomach and ample breasts. The bottom was a very short miniskirt with a longer train in the back. The six-inch heels she wore gave her legs a defined look and Koko loved the outcome. She wore her hair in a bun with a few curls hanging on the sides. The diamond chandelier earrings and matching choker put the finishing touch on her style.

It was time to go out and be seen. Right on cue, there was a knock on the door. Koko grabbed the black clutch and put her phone and room key inside before walking out of the bedroom. The knocking became louder as Horace became impatient on the other side.

Koko swung the door open with a grimaced expression, but it turned into a big smile when she laid eyes on her friend. She was used to seeing him in his flamboyant outfits and man purses. Not that night though. Horace was standing in the doorway looking like a million bucks dressed in a black double-breasted tuxedo. He was clean as a whistle and Koko was very impressed.

"Look at you!" She said happily. "I was prepared to see a little pink somewhere in your getup. You clean up well, friend."

"Oh, I have pink on for sure. Some man will have the privilege of removing my pink thong with ease at the end of the night," Horace winked. "I may be gay but baby I know how to play the role as well. When you're in the presence of money, the gaydar becomes very useful. These types of men are deep in the closet, but Horace knows how to spot 'em, girl. I'm not coming back to this hotel alone. Even if they want to keep the shit on the low; I'm with it."

"You're a mess." Koko laughed. "You look good though. Let's get out of here so we won't be late. I already know traffic is about to be terrible."

They stepped onto the elevator and it didn't stop until they reached the garage floor. Soon as they exited, Koko's phone rang inside her clutch. Walking toward her car she pulled it out and looked at the screen. Stephan's name appeared and she smiled before pushing the call button to connect the call.

"Mr. McCormick, I'm getting in my truck as we speak. I'll be there shortly, depending on traffic."

"No, you don't have to drive. There's a car waiting outside the hotel to escort you to the event. Nothing but the best for a beautiful woman as yourself."

"Oh, that was nice of you. Thank you so much. I'll see you in a bit, Mr. McCormick."

"See you then, beautiful," Stephan said ending the call.

Koko turned and walked back to the elevator while Horace watched confused. "Um, the truck is that way," he said pointing his thumb behind him.

"I know. It seems as if I don't have to drive to the event. Stephan sent a car for us and the driver is waiting in front of the hotel."

"Yeah, that man is sweet on you." He smirked.

"No, he's not! This is business and he's just looking out for me. I told you I'm not here to mingle with these muthafuckas on a personal level. You're thinking too much into what it's not, Horace." Koko stepped into the elevator soon as the doors opened.

"If you say so. That man likes you and it's not because you did the damn thang with his creation either. Watch what

I tell you. Mr. McCormick is going to make his move tonight."

"Whatever."

Horace followed behind Koko as her heels clacked across the floor of the lobby. When they made their way out of the hotel entrance doors both of them stopped in their tracks. There was a black man in a suit holding a sign that read: *Kameeko Simmons +1*. Behind him a Midnight black Rolls Royce was parked with the back door open.

"Bitch, is that a Rolls?" Horace whispered in her ear.

"Yup. It's so pretty."

She walked in the direction of the driver with a smile. When he looked down at her, his eyes roamed her body before giving her face the attention it should've received first. He glanced at the sign and back at Koko.

"Miss Simmons?"

"Yes. Good evening, Sir."

"I'm Patrick. I'll be your driver tonight. You're beautiful by the way."

"Thank you." Koko blushed.

Patrick took Koko by the hand escorting her into the expensive vehicle. He stepped back and allowed Horace to join her before closing the door. Koko glanced around taking in the interior of the car and fell in love with it. One day she would be able to afford one of her own. She mentally put custom Rolls Royce on her bucket list. Koko was going to work her ass off to scratch everything off of it before she turned thirty. At twenty-six years old, four years was a stretch, but she was more determined than ever to make the shit happen.

"Oh, yeah, boo, I gots to get my hand on one of these rich niggas. I want to live the life like the Jeffersons. It's time to move up to the East side. To the deluxe apartments in the sky. We finally got a piece of the pie."

Koko fell out laughing because Horace was being his humorous self. Patrick sat in the driver seat and looked into the rearview mirror. He stared at Koko long and hard before starting the vehicle.

"There are drinks in the fridge. Help yourself to whatever. It's all there for you all to enjoy. I'm going to give you two some privacy."

"Thank you, Patrick," Koko said with a smile. "Horace, pour us a drink."

Horace didn't waste a moment opening the mini fridge to see what was in store for them. There were bottles of champagne, Remy, Hennessy, and tequila chilling in the there. Horace chose the champagne and Koko was happy about his choice. She didn't want to get fucked up before she could get to the venue. It wouldn't be professional of her to be slurring while trying to mingle with the people she planned to have invest in her company.

They had about fifteen minutes minimum before they were expected to reach the venue. Koko took the flute from Horace and took a sip. The conversation Koko had with Jackie's mom came to mind. She turned to Horace and shook her head.

"What's wrong?"

"I had to called Jackie's mama today."

"For what?" he asked with furrowed brows.

"She had the nerve to call me. I had to let her ass know she was a sorry muthafucka before parting her lips to apologize."

"You do know Jackie is only sorry because she wants something, right?"

"I do and I told her just that. She fucked up with me. There's no coming back from what she did to me. Jackie's mama knows all about the fight at the club. I asked her to talk with her and let her daughter know not to contact me again. Bad as I wanted to dog her out, I didn't. I just want Jackie to leave me the fuck alone before I whoop her ass again."

"Going to her mama only pissed her off more. She is going to retaliate because you told her business. What you should've done was told her mama that Jackie is sleeping with Cyrus," Horace smirked.

"We don't know if that's true or not. I would never spread false information unless I have concrete evidence. If they are messing around, Miss Stella is going to be the one to make both of them feel bad about what they had done. Me on the other hand couldn't care less."

"You're better than me, Koko. I would be going to see what's really going on between them because I would want to know."

"Good thing I don't give a fuck, right? Like I've stated before, I have more important things to worry about."

"It's obvious the shit is bothering you. Otherwise, you wouldn't be thinking about the call or how you had to involve Jackie's mother."

The situation truly bothered Koko and trying to deny it wouldn't work with Horace because he knew her fairly well. His bluntness made her feel like such a fool at times but when he talked, he spoke the truth. It was time to put all of the bullshit behind her because the vehicle stopped in front of the venue prompting Koko to down the rest of her drink. Horace grabbed her hand giving it a gently squeeze.

"I am so proud of you, Koko. From the first day I met you, then I started working for you, and fell in love with the person you are inside and out. Your drive has always been top tier, but now, you are a force to be reckoned with. You are going over and beyond with the projects you create and the recognition you are about to receive has been a long time in the making. I want you to keep striving to be the best in what you do. And I will be here the entire way through."

"Awwww, thank you, Horace. I appreciate that so much. If things go my way, you and others will be on my payroll. With you being my COO. You will go wherever I go without hesitations. So, I hope you are ready for what's in store for Koko Kakes & More."

"I'm here for it. Where you go, I go."

The door opened and Patrick stepped to the side so Horace could exit. He stepped forward to assist Koko out by once again reaching out for her hand. Koko automatically shot Horace a look to keep his thoughts to himself. He understood the assignment even though he had to bite the inside of his jaw to stay quiet. Koko thanked Patrick and made her way along the red carpet leading into the venue. The host at the door held a clipboard in her hand. She asked for their names then allowed them entrance once she crossed it off the list. Koko was also told what table she was assigned to sit.

Whoever did the decorations had done an amazing job. They were led into a large ballroom that was filled with many tables draped in black tablecloths with crystal dinnerware perfectly placed. Koko became nervous as she took in the utensils because she didn't know the difference between the two forks. She had never been to an event of that caliber and didn't want to feel dumb for not knowing. Horace must've read her thoughts because he hugged her shoulder.

"We got this. You won't go into this blindly with me by your side. I've taken plenty of etiquette classes to prepare for moments like this. I have you to thank for putting me in the room to showcase what I've learned."

Koko smiled and relaxed. The atmosphere was totally different from the bottle popping club parties she was accustomed to attending. The live band was soothing to the soul and brought a calm aura to Koko's mind. She looked around for Stephan and didn't see him anywhere. Instead of sitting like a duck, she searched for the table she was assigned. When she found it, she sat bouncing her leg nervously.

"Girl, why are you so nervous?" Horace asked sitting next to her. "This is your time to shine. You better get up and introduce yourself to these people. Did you bring business cards? Networking is key."

Chewing on her bottom lip, Koko silence told him all he needed to know. She forgot. Horace stood going into his pocket. He produced a stack of business cards and handed them to his boss.

"Put these in your clutch." When Koko did what she was told, Horace produced another stack, giving her half. "I got your back. Now get your mind right and let's go talk business. You work one side of the room, and I got the other. We, together, are Koko Kakes & More. You ready?"

Reading over the business card brought tears to Koko's eyes. Horace had updated them and she loved what he had done. The cards were very professional with her logo and picture on full display. Koko would've been writing her information on napkins if Horace hadn't come through for her. Folks would have thought she was a joke for sure. Giving him a tight hug, Koko stepped back blinking rapidly to stop the tears.

"Thank you. I love them. You are a life saver, boo."

"This is a happy moment. We are not crying tonight." Horace said glancing across the room. "I see some eye candy. I need to get over there to see if my gaydar is going to go berserk in his presence. We will meet back up later, or you come find me. If you don't see me, hit my line because I may be hiding out somewhere on my knees."

"Horace, you better not embarrass me in here." Koko cut her eyes at him.

"Embarrass? Baby, I'm about to open the floodgates for your business. This throat is lethal. You will thank me later because there are a lot of men here that likes my kind. I can feel the energy in the room," he smirked. "Catch me outside. How 'bout that?"

Horace sauntered off with his head held high and business cards in hand. Koko couldn't do anything but laugh at his antics. She had to love his crazy ass though. As she walked through the room Koko spotted Stephan talking to someone by the stage on the other side. She made her way to who she was familiar with. As she got closer, Stephan smiled as he watched her approach. He said something to the man standing before him nodding at her. The man turned around and Koko's breath caught in her throat.

"Kameeko, I would like for you to meet..."

"Kazimir," she whispered, licking her lips.

Stephan looked from Koko to Kazimir with confusion. The two were not in the same circle and he wondered how they knew one another. It didn't take long to find out. Kazimir smiled as he admired her in the lovely gown she wore. She was just as beautiful than she was the night he carried her out of the club after fighting. Koko was in professional mode and like himself, she hid the other persona of herself well. There were two sides to the woman he couldn't stop thinking about and he wanted to get to know her on every level.

"Kameeko, nice to see you again. I guess fate is real, huh? There's a reason we were put in the same room once again. How have you been?"

"It's nice to see you as well, Mr...."

"Aht, aht. We not about to go into pleasantries. It's Kazimir or Kaz. Whichever one you prefer," he said, licking his lips. "Stephan was just telling me how talented you were. I've learned more about you from him than I heard from the woman herself."

"That's only because we met under different circumstances. Maybe we were meant to meet again to discuss what we both do on a professional level."

"I'm going to allow you two to talk privately for a moment. Kameeko, do you have any business cards on you? I've spoken your name to quite a few people tonight, and I want them to be able to get in touch with you in the future," Stephan stated.

"Sure, take these. I have more in my clutch. Thank you so much, Mr. McCormick. I really appreciate you."

"No problem," he said giving Kaz a knowingly glance. "Behave yourself, Mr. St. Claire."

Kaz was glad Nicolette decided not to attend the event with him. She was still in her feelings about his truth, but he didn't care about all that. What he was interested in was Kameeko looking good enough to eat standing in front of him. They stared each other down for what seemed like forever before Koko broke the silence.

"Mr. St. Claire, huh? Could you be related to the owner of St. Claire's Candies?"

"Yes, that would be my grandfather. What you know about that?"

"I grew up on the candy. I would always sneak to the store just to grab some. I've never been to the actual warehouse though. Can you get me in? The caramel is my favorite."

"Well, the original warehouse isn't active anymore. After I took over the company…"

"You're the new owner of St. Claire's candies?" Koko surprisingly asked.

Kaz chuckled. "Yes. I took over almost three years ago when my grandfather fell ill. I moved the company to Michigan Avenue. We are now located on the top floor of the Water Tower place. We make fresh candy and also sell from that location."

"That's so dope! I'm sorry about Mr. St. Claire. My condolences."

"No. No. My grandfather is alive and well. He's just not in the best health to run the business anymore."

"Oh, my apologies. Well, tell him he has a fan in me. I've always wanted to meet the man behind my favorite candy. I haven't had any since I moved four years ago. I plan to stock up before I leave though."

"How long will you be in town?"

"I'm leaving on Monday. Why do you ask?" Koko wondered.

"Maybe I want to gift you some caramels. Is that alright with you?"

"No, you don't have to do that. I'm more than capable of purchasing the candy myself. I'm an entrepreneur too so I know how important it is for people to pay for the business provided."

"See, Koko, that's where you're wrong. I don't care about the money per se. It's the glimmer of happiness in your eyes when you speak on the candy for me. It would be my way of thanking you for loving my grandfather's creation. Please don't fight me over something so small."

"It seems I won't win this battle. You're going to do whatever you want. It seems your mind is already made up," Koko shrugged.

She looked around for Horace and saw him talking to a man in the corner with a glass of Champagne in his hand. Her assistant seemed to be enjoying himself while Koko hadn't moved from the first spot she stopped. She felt like a failure to her own company because she wasn't working the room as planned. Koko smiled at Kaz and placed her hand on his shoulder.

"I have to end this conversation. There are so many potential clients in the room, and I need to try my hand at getting to them. It was nice seeing you again, Mr. St. Claire. Take care of yourself and keep doing what you're doing with your business." Koko turned to walk away, but Kaz grabbed her arm before she could take a step.

"For the last time, call me Kaz or Kazimir. It's going to be hell to pay if the only time you're calling me what I prefer is when I'm caressing the silky walls of your pussy," he whispered. "Don't say shit in return, Koko. I do whatever I want, remember. Your words, not mine. I'll see you later, Koko."

Kaz kissed her on the cheek then walked away. Koko stood frozen in place as the softness of his lips lingered on her skin. She watched as Kaz and Stephan talked before she was pulled away by the sound of a woman's voice.

"He is handsome, isn't he?" she asked.

Koko forced a smile at the woman and shook her head to clear the nasty thoughts from her mind. The older woman was beautiful, and Koko didn't know who she was. Trying to find her voice, Koko failed and nodded instead of answering verbally. Recognition kicked in and Koko remember exactly who the woman was. It was Sophie Morales, a news anchor for WGN news. The nerves she thought were gone came back with a vengeance. Koko didn't think the media would be in attendance. The last thing she wanted was her family to see that she was in Chicago.

"I'm Sophie Morales."

"I know exactly who you are. Nice to meet you." Koko smiled, holding out her hand.

"You are Kameeko Simmons, correct?"

Again, Koko nodded.

"I've heard nothing but great things about you. I can't wait to see the display of your work. If it's as good as they say it is, you will get a slot on my segment tonight."

"Oh, wow," Koko said nervously. "Thank you very much."

"You're very welcome," Sophie said as her attention went to the stage. "As a matter of fact, I'm about to find out right now. Do you have a business card? I'm being summoned to the stage."

Koko handed Sophie a business card then made her way to the table she was assigned to. Stephan walked on the stage and stopped to talk to the media. He took his place at the microphone clearing his throat before addressing the crowd.

"I would like everyone to take your seats. We will be unveiling the first look of my new locomotive then soon after, dinner will be served."

The cart Koko provided for the display was rolled onto the stage and her heart started beating fast in her chest. Her anxiety was at an all-time high as she pictured the curtain falling and her creation was destroyed. She hadn't seen the piece since she put it on the truck back in Minnesota. Koko only had the word of Stephan that it was fine the day she arrived in Chicago. She worked hard to perfect the replica of the real locomotive. Koko wanted her work to be seen. No, she needed it to be seen by everyone. She had so much riding on the moment.

Horace sat next to her, grabbed her hand and squeezed it, trying to give her reassurance that everything was alright because she looked so afraid. "Are you okay, friend?" he asked concerned.

Beads of sweat formed on Koko's forehead, and she was extremely hot even though the air was on full blast in the venue. Horace poured her a glass of ice water and placed the straw to her lips. Taking a long sip, Koko drank half of the liquid before she stopped to take a breath. At that moment, Kazimir walked over and kneeled on the side of her. Horace watched his every move as he cupped his friend's chin turning her head to look at him.

"You got this, beautiful. There's nothing for you to worry about. Do you trust that you have done your best with this project?"

Koko nodded because she couldn't find her voice for shit.

"Then you got this. If you don't believe in yourself nobody else will either. Tighten up, Queen. I want you to know, I believe in you."

He pulled up a chair and sat right next to her. Horace watched Koko's body relax under the mystery man's presence. He wondered who the man was but glad his friend was out of the panic attack zone. She would have to fill him in once they left the venue because that man was more than an acquaintance. The way he looked at Koko said he wanted to feel on her booty real bad. Stephan's voice brought everybody's attention to the stage.

"As everyone knows, I've upgraded my freight for Renaissance Railroads. I had the liberty of meeting a talented young woman who specializes in chocolate sculpting. She also makes cakes and anything else you would want baked. Kameeko Simmons is her name, and she is the creator of this lovely piece. You may also remember her from the hit show *Finding the Next Best Chocolatier*. Kameeko walked away with the grand prize, and she is also the owner of Koko's Kakes & More.

"Kameeko is a Chicago Native who resides in Minnesota. A college graduate who is doing very well for herself in a world that doesn't recognize the greatness of our black Kings and Queens. I'm not one of those people. So, Kameeko, come up to the stage, please. You should be standing next to me during this reveal."

Koko looked at Horace with fear in her eyes. She mouthed, "I can't go up there," to him.

Kaz sat watching her with his eyebrows furrowed. It was a pivotal moment for her, and he wasn't about to allow her to miss out on it. Taking her hand in his, Kaz stood from his seat forcing Koko out of hers. He took a step, but she didn't move which irritated him. "Kameeko, this is your time to shine, ma. You have to do this. What are you afraid of?" he asked lowly.

"My family will see this," she said, biting her bottom lip.

"So. They should be proud of your accomplishments."

"You don't understand, Kazimir."

"And you can tell me all about it after you accept your recognition. Stephan has already mentioned you. They already know. You may as well give them something to talk about. If they're not there for you in everything you decide to do; fuck 'em. I'm here and I'm not going anywhere."

Kaz hugged her and the cameras zoomed in on them. He released her body but held on to her hand as he guided her to the stage. Koko's hand was clammy but that didn't bother him one bit. Every step Koko took, every man in the room took in her beauty. Once she stood next to Stephan, Koko avoided the cameras much as she could. He hugged her and smiled.

"This woman here is the next rising star. I believe in what she has done, and you will too. With that being said, it is time to reveal this masterpiece made by hand in five hundred seventy-six hours. If that's not dedication, I don't know what is," Stephan continued to praise Koko and her hard work. "I'm here to present the first look of the upgraded locomotive of Renaissance Railroad."

Stephan motioned for the workers to unveil the piece, and the gasps and applause was deafening. The standing ovation Koko received brought tears to her eyes. She had created a lot of memorable pieces but she never received that type of feedback in her life. Knowing people all over had seen what her hands could do made her proud of herself.

Seeing her work on display took all the thoughts of being seen on television away instantly. She admired the locomotive with pride and the tears flowed. *Celebration* by Kool & the Gang blared through the speakers as confetti fell from the ceiling. Koko was actually being praised for something she put her heart and soul into completing. Sophie came on stage and stuck a microphone in her face.

Koko was uncomfortable, but she answered every question with her head held high. When the questions about family entered the chat, Kazimir noticed her discomfort and led her away. He guided Koko out of the venue to get a breath of fresh air.

"You did great, ma. That train is the shit, too!"

"Thank you. I'm so glad it's over." Koko chuckled.

"Nah, this is just the beginning. There's more in store for you, Kameeko. Keep your phone on because the calls are going to start rolling in probably tomorrow. If there is anything I can help with, do not hesitate to give me a call,"

Kaz said. "I'm going to be the first person to sponsor your company. Stephan will come at you next. It won't stop there. Things are about to be surreal until you get used to being in the spotlight."

"Oh my God! I'm not going to know the first thing about handling success of this magnitude."

"Don't worry. I'll be there every step of the way. You have my word on that. Now, I'm hungry. We need to go back inside because the menu is one for the books and I don't want to miss out on that."

Koko laughed and turned so they could go back inside. Horace stood by the door waiting for his friend. He gave her a high five and hugged her tight.

"We did that, boo! They love you and your magical hands."

"I didn't do it alone. You came through in the clutch. Thank you." Koko smiled at Horace because things were definitely about to change for them. "Are you ready to step into the role of being my COO?"

"I accepted that position before you became famous. So, my decision is still the same. If you rockin', I'm rollin'."

"Bet. We will discuss it more later. Until then, it's time to eat and celebrate us."

They approached the table and there were six other people sitting. The table was set for nine and everyone clapped, while congratulating Koko as she sat down. Except one woman who looked to have an attitude. Koko didn't think nothing of it, but Horace did. He was always on top of all upcoming drama, and it never went unnoticed with him around.

"Who is that?" he asked lowly.

"I don't know." Koko said looking around for Kazimir.

She spotted him by the door carrying on a conversation with someone. When she turned back the woman was snarling at her. Koko didn't know the woman from a can of paint. In fact, she had never seen the woman before in her life. She tried her best to go back in time through memory to figure out if she had gone to school with her. Nothing clicked. A server came over with a cart of salad when Kazimir joined the table. He sat next to the woman without even a hello so, that told Koko he didn't know who the woman was either.

"Kazimir, I hope you have been enjoying your night thus far," she said putting a forkful of salad in her mouth.

"Nicolette, I thought you weren't coming."

"I changed my mind. Who is your little friend?" she asked gesturing toward Koko.

"An acquaintance. Don't start your shit tonight. I will have you escorted the fuck out of here," he said low enough for only Nicolette to hear.

"Does she know you're married while you doing all the extra for her as if she's your woman? Yeah, I've been here long enough and seen it all."

Koko listened to the back and forth between Kazimir and the woman she now knew as Nicolette. She didn't like where things were going because she had no clue he was married. Plus, they hadn't done anything inappropriate for her to assume otherwise. It wasn't Koko's place to set things straight, so she kept her mouth shut. Kazimir would have to handle whatever problem his wife had because he didn't want Koko to.

"I don't care what you *thought* you saw, but you are wrong on every level. We will not do this here." Kaz snarled.

"Fine. Since you won't tell me what I need to know, maybe she will."

Nicolette turned her attention to Koko and all eyes at the table were on the two of them. She had just experienced a very special moment of her life and here comes this woman trying to take her back to the streets. Koko had to constantly remind herself that she was not in the hood. She was surrounded by classy, intelligent, and rich individuals. Her actions from that day forward had to be on point. She had a lot riding on her future.

"No, ma'am. I won't," Koko said shaking her head. "I met Kazimir tonight just like everyone else I've spoken with in this room. It's business for me. Nothing more, nothing less. What you witnessed when your husband hugged me, was him reassuring me that I would be okay on the stage. If there is turmoil in your marriage, it has absolutely nothing to do with me. Leave me out of whatever bullshit you have conjured up in your mind."

"But did he tell you he had a wife and kid at home?" Nicolette pushed.

"In fact, he did. He actually spoke quite fondly about his daughter." Koko lied while sprinkling a little bit of shade along the way. "I'm not the woman you should be trying to figure out. The person who has you questioning your husband's faithfulness is not sitting at this table. I would advise one thing though, don't ever pan me out to being a homewrecker. That's not my style."

"There's women out here that's sleeping with my husband…"

"And I'm not one of them." Koko snarled. "Your insecurities are going to be the reason this man sitting next to you is going to walk away. No one wants to be accused of cheating every time they are in the presence of a woman. You should try working on your low self-esteem because you're going to approach the wrong woman with your accusations, and it's not going to go the way you thought it would. With that being said, don't say anything else to me. Capeesh?"

Kaz had enough. He grabbed Nicolette by the arm and escorted her out of the venue. When they were far away from the door, he turned her loose. The way he glared at her kind of frightened Nicolette. His eyes were dark as night and his jawline was chiseled. She had never seen him so upset. She knew upsetting him in front of his peers were the wrong thing to do, but she needed answers to why he was so comfortable with the beautiful chocolate beauty sitting at the table.

"What the fuck is your problem?"

"I don't have one. How would you feel if you walked into a room and I was all over a man the way you were with her?"

"To be honest, I would be relieved. At least I would know you are out trying to enjoy yourself as I've suggested many times. You just sat in there and made a fool of your damn self. What I was doing for her was pure innocence. She was nervous and I was there to make sure she carried herself like a black queen. Nothing more."

"But you told her about Alessia. What's that about?" she asked. "I thought you weren't going to bring our daughter up to your hoes."

"I don't fuck with hoes, Nicolette. I deal with women who can suck my dick like a vacuum and swallow the kids I have no intentions of producing with them. Then they go home not worrying about who else I'm fucking while they sleep soundly in their own beds."

"You are one disrespectful motherfucker! If you don't want to be my husband, divorce me, Kazimir."

"I never wanted to be your husband. Must I keep reminding you why we are at this point in our lives? You want to talk divorce, huh? You draw up the papers and I will sign them bitches, no questions asked. I'm not initiating shit because I'm going to live my life however, I see fit whether you like it or not. You're the one throwing tantrums because you aren't happy. My life goes on with or without you. Now, Alessia is a different story."

Nicolette cried silently as she listened to Kazimir read her down. He has stated how he felt for years and his storyline never changed. There was no way she could win his love because he had zero to give. At least for her anyway. She hated the fact he put her daughter above everything they were going through. Nicolette had to admit she was jealous of Alessia because the love she wanted from Kazimir; her daughter was getting it one hundred percent.

"I'll see you at home. I'm leaving."

"Bye," Kaz said watching her walk away to find her car.

Kaz headed for the entrance of the venue and stopped. Koko's comeback was amazing to him. She didn't allow Nicolette and her antics get her out of character and he was proud of her for that. She even amazed him by hitting the nail on the coffin without knowing when she mentioned him talking about Alessia when he hadn't. He could tell that alone bothered Nicolette, but she brought the shit on herself. Kaz was more worried about how Koko was going to react toward him once he was back in her presence. *There was only one way to find out*, he thought as he made his way back inside.

Chapter 9

Cyrus was sitting in the trap after having a conversation with Lowkey. He was told the trap ran by Bird had come up short not once but twice in the matter of two weeks. That wasn't Cyrus' neck of the woods and had nothing to do with him because his shit was straight. He just didn't like when the nigga in charge decided he wanted to come through trying to check him about something that didn't concern him. After giving Lowkey a piece of his mind, Cyrus told him to get the fuck out of his face with the bullshit. Whoever put his ass in charge was stupid because Lowkey was softer than room temperature butter.

He made sure his workers were on their business before turning on the television to see what crimes were being broadcasted on the news. Cyrus had just missed a segment about an accident on highway 35W but was just in time to watch the feature about a new business owner. He looked over at the door just as Austin walked in. Cyrus didn't address him because he was still tight about Austin telling his business.

"What's up, Cy?"

"Shit. You ready to reup?" he asked with his eyes on the T.V.

"Yeah."

Cyrus got up and went to the back room to grab the work he'd prepacked for Austin. Making sure everything was there. He turned the light off as his name was called from the other room. Austin was too excited about whatever he wanted so that made Cyrus pick up his pace.

"Aye, that's the nigga who carried Koko out of the club," Austin said pointing to the screen. "I still don't know who he is, but it seems like he is right by her side in Chicago."

Koko told Cyrus she didn't fuck that nigga, but they seemed very comfortable standing next to each other in front of all those rich muthafuckas. His girl looked good as hell. The dress she had on was beautiful. She was showing too much skin for his liking but what pissed him off the most was the way the nigga had his arm around her waist. Cyrus listened to what was being said and his mouth fell to the floor. Koko was doing big things and he was proud of her.

The owner of Renaissance Railroads was praising his girl and that was one hell of an accomplishment. When they unveiled Koko's replica of the locomotive, Cyrus couldn't do anything but smile. One thing he couldn't do was discredit her talent. Koko was always cold when it came to bringing a chocolate sculpture to life. He never thought she would make it any bigger than the T.V. show she was on, but he was obviously wrong.

"She fuckin' that nigga," Austin blurted.

"Nah, she's not. I need you to mind yo' business when it comes to her though. What she does is my issue, not yours. Are we clear?"

"My bad, dawg. Ya'll ain't together anyway so why does it matter?"

"Man, raise the fuck up. I'm about to head out."

Cyrus turned the television off then headed for the door. He handed the pack to Austin, retrieved his payment for the week, and basically pushed him out of the front door of the trap. He hollered at his workers about what he expected then got in his whip. Cyrus started the engine but didn't pull out of the parking spot. Instead, he grabbed his phone and dialed Koko's number. When she didn't answer, Cyrus became angry. He tried again getting the same result so, he sent her a text.

Cyrus: I saw you on the news and wanted to say congratulations. I saw you with that nigga from the club too. Soon as I find out who he is, I'm going to let him know you mine.

The bubbles were going wild on his screen then they stopped. Cyrus waited a few minutes for Koko's response but when it didn't come, he put the car in gear and pulled away from the curb. He was driving toward his apartment when his phone rang. He didn't bother looking to see who was calling when he answered. Cyrus assumed it was Koko calling instead of texting so he didn't even say hello.

"Cyrus, are you okay?" Sheree's voice filled the interior of the car.

"I'm good. What's up?"

"CJ wanted to say goodnight before going to bed."

He hadn't been to Sheree's in a few weeks because she was on bullshit about what happened between, she and Koko. Cyrus wasn't about to go back and forth with her about an incident she had caused. Sheree wanted to question him about his relationship with Koko. He wasn't obligated to answer anything because for one, Sheree wasn't his woman. She was just his baby mama. Two, she knew what the fuck it was when she involved herself with him. And lastly, she was still going to suck his dick and fuck whenever he wanted her to so she could just shut up trying to act like she had a position. The only thing Cyrus needed Sheree to do was take care of her son. All the other shit she could keep.

"I'll slide through for a quick minute since he will be sleep soon after or before I even get there."

"Okay," Sheree said hanging up.

Cyrus knew she didn't waste time ending the call because she was hopping in the shower before he arrived. Sheree was hurting her own feelings though. He had already dried his nuts up for the day. All he was going to do was kiss his son goodnight then take his ass home to get some sleep. That alone was going to cause an argument, and he wasn't in the mood for it. Maybe he would eat her pussy to keep her quiet. He'd see what happened when he got to her crib. Stopping at a red light, Cyrus picked his phone up again and sent another message to Koko since she failed to respond to the previous one.

Cyrus: You read my message, started to reply, and didn't. Stop fuckin' playing with me Koko. I don't give a fuck what we go through. We forever. That nigga bet not be with you at this time of night. Disrespecting me is not something you want to do right now. Make me hit the road.

The message was delivered then read popped up underneath it. Cyrus' nose flared when Koko didn't start typing. He was about to put the phone down when it rang in his hand. He was about five minutes away from Sheree's so he answered the call.

"Why are you playing games, Koko?"

"I'm not playing shit. I figured I would call so you wouldn't get what I'm about to say misconstrued. Cyrus, you are not scaring nobody except the bitch you had a baby with. I'm not the one or the muthafuckin' two. We ain't nothing. I told you what it was over a month ago. We are done; since you don't recall the conversation we had. It doesn't matter if Jesus himself is with me in this hotel room, it's not your business. Do you, and I'm damn sure gonna do me. Please don't call my phone talking out the side of your neck because you didn't know what to do with me when you had me!"

Koko ended the call without saying goodbye. The only reason she called was to speak her mind and she did that. Cyrus could feel however he wanted because her narrative would not change. In the Benz he was driving, Cyrus had to laugh in order to continue on to his destination instead of jumping on the highway to Chicago. Koko had to come back to the Twin Cities and she was definitely going to see him for trying to play him like some sucka ass nigga.

Cyrus' attitude was on ten when he pulled into Sheree's driveway. The shit Koko said had him ready to wring her neck. He had to remind himself that he didn't put his hands on women. Her slick ass mouth was going to make him forget for a split second just to slap her in that muthafucka one good time. Using his key to gain entry, the smell of vanilla scented candles met him at the door. Slow jams could be heard coming from upstairs and Cyrus shook his head. He already knew what his baby mama was on. The way he felt at the point, Cyrus needed to release his frustration in order to calm down. Sheree was about to get the business.

Climbing the stairs, Cyrus went down the hall to the left when he got to the top of the landing. He had to check on his shorty before anything else could pop off. Cyrus pushed the door open taking in the sight of tiny dinosaurs bouncing off the walls from the night light on the dresser. Cj was curled in his bed with his thumb in his mouth. Cyrus didn't like the habit his son picked up since he was born. Teeth was going to be fucked up by the time he reached the third grade. Leaning down beside the bed, Cyrus removed Cj's thumb from his mouth.

"No, daddy, give it back. I need that," Cj whined putting his thumb right back in his mouth.

"I love you, lil dude," Cyrus said kissing his son on the top of his head.

"I luh u too, daddy." Cj snuggled under the covers without opening his eyes.

Cyrus chuckled because his son knew it was him without even seeing him. He was the only person that tried to keep Cj from sucking his thumb. Cyrus was always on him about it but no matter what, Cj was going to do what he had grown to do from birth. Cyrus was ready to pay top dollar to correct his teeth when the time came to do so.

Leaving his son's room, Cyrus pulled the door up behind him then went looking for Sheree's hot ass. He didn't have to look far because she stood naked than the day she was born in the doorway of her bedroom. Cyrus mans swelled up in his pants causing him to cup it with his hand.

"Why you out here with yo' ass out, girl? You didn't know if my son would be in my arms or not."

"I was waiting on you. Cj hates to be disturbed while he's sleeping. You and I both knows that." She smirked seductively.

"I didn't come here for this shit, but you look too damn good to pass up."

Cyrus lifted Sheree into his arms as he kissed the side of her neck. He kicked the door closed then placed her back against the wall. Cyrus used his muscular arms to hoist her up by the ass while her glistening lower lips stared him in the face. For him not to be on anything sexual, his mouth salivated instantly from the scent of her sweet essence. He dove in headfirst wrapping his lips around her pearl.

"Aaaaw, shit!"

Sheree palmed his head as she ground her kitty against his mouth. Her stomach muscles clenched, then she came long and hard. Sheree called Cyrus the head doctor because he was skilled with his tongue.

"That's enough," she moaned, pushing at his head. "I can't take anymore."

Ignoring her pleas, Cyrus stuck his tongue deep inside her pussy. He had to clean up the mess he'd made. Sheree's juices moisturized the small stubble of hair on his chin. Cupping her ass, he carried Sheree to the bed, gently lying her down. Her chest rose and fell as she tried catching her breath. The flickers of the candles danced around the room giving off a sexual glow. Cyrus pulled his shirt over his head slowly as Sheree took in his tatted chest. She loved every one of them except the one that said *Kameeko* over his heart. It was the first time she actually paid attention to the script. She wanted to tell him to have the tattoo removed but didn't want to mess up the vibe. Instead, Sheree ran her fingers up and down her slit as she watched him step out of the joggers he wore. His meat sprang out like a strong slinky.

"Why you outside with no draws on?"

"So, I won't struggle to release this muthafucka. He popped out with ease, now come over here and let me see what that mouth do." He smirked.

Sheree wasted no time repositioning herself on the bed. She laid on her back as her head hung from the edge of the bed. Cyrus knew what time it was and had no problem feeding her the dick. With every suckle his toes curled in his shoes. Sheree took his entire shaft into her throat gagging every so often. She wasn't a pro like Koko, but her performance would do.

Closing his eyes, Cyrus envisioned the love of his life as his baby mama pleasured him. He felt the sensation of his nut trying to get the best of him and took a step back. The popping sound of Sheree's lips caused him to smile.

"Why did you do that?" She pouted.

"I got more for you. If you want this to be over quickly, I'll bring it back. If not, turn around and put that ass in the air. I want a deep arch too."

Sheree assumed the position and waited for Cyrus to take her from behind. He thought about putting on a condom but that didn't last long. Cyrus wanted to feel every part of her walls without the barrier. He smacked one of her cheeks hard making Sheree's ass jiggle before entering her slowly. Pausing for a moment to take in her tightness, Cyrus grabbed her waist and went to work. Sheree bounced back trying to match his strokes.

"Fuck, Cyrus!" Sheree moaned, falling forward.

"Throw that ass, Ree. Don't tap out just yet. Bring that ass back."

He pulled her toward him and reached around to her wet center. Cyrus strummed her bud as he pumped in and out of her yoni. Sheree was in a euphoric bliss. She had to mentally remind herself that the act they were performing wasn't long term. It was always temporary when it came to, she and Cyrus. Whenever they had intercourse, Sheree cherished the time because it wasn't often, they would be in each other's presence in that way.

Cyrus' strokes quickened as his orgasm built up. He got lost in the moment as he closed his eyes to concentrate on the nut he was about to let loose. Koko entered his mind and he wanted to give her a baby so she would love him again.

"Arrrrghhhh!" he growled as he released his seeds deep inside Sheree. "You gon' have my baby, Koko?"

Sheree moved out of the way faster than a speeding bullet. She rolled to the farthest side of the bed as she glared at Cyrus. He stood with cum dripping from the tip of his dick as if he didn't just call her another woman's name. Sheree knew he wasn't her man, but she'd be damned if she was disrespected in the process.

"Why would you move?"

"Are you serious? Did you hear what the fuck you said out your mouth? My name is not Koko and her name shouldn't have been the one falling from your lips. Get the fuck out of my house, Cyrus. You want that bitch so bad, go fuck her!"

"My bad. I apologize for what happened. It wasn't my intention to say that. I was caught up in the moment."

"How the hell did you get caught up by calling out her name while deep inside of me?" Sheree hissed. "You must think I'm boo boo the fool or somebody. Koko is on your mind. Go be with her, Cyrus."

Sheree got out of the bed and walked right out of the bedroom. Cyrus stood in the same spot feeling like an ass. Not only did he come over to Sheree's and have sex with her, he had also fucked someone else before her. To make things worse, he called out the woman's name that pissed him off right before stepping foot in the house. Yeah, he needed to leave because he had messed up big time. There was nothing more Cyrus could do other than admit he was wrong.

Pulling up his pants then threw his shirt over his head, Cyrus walked out of the bedroom to find Sheree. He could hear the water running in the bathroom down the hall and followed the sound. When he twisted the doorknob, it was locked. Cyrus knocked but his baby mama didn't respond.

"Sheree, I'm sorry. I'm going to head out. I hope you would forgive me for what I did."

Cyrus walked away from the door and headed down the stairs. The stress with the women in his life was going to be the death of him. He had to leave everybody alone and concentrate on Koko since that was what his mind focused on. Cyrus was ready to do just that. Soon as he got word of Koko being back in Minnesota.

Chapter 10

The sparks ignited between Koko and Kazimir until his wife showed up, then it fizzled on Koko's end. She didn't want to seem standoffish but that was exactly what happened when he came back inside alone. Koko couldn't be mad at him for not mentioning he had a wife because they really hadn't sat down to discuss their lives with one another. Finding out he was a taken man before anything could transpire between them was best in her opinion. Better sooner than later because they could still be friends if nothing else.

Koko was still able to enjoy the rest of the party. She met so many prominent people that were willing to sponsor her company to get it further off the ground. Koko was grateful for all Stephan had done for her. The mere thought of a complete stranger believing in her the way he had was a Godsend. Being in the same room as wealthy entrepreneurs was a dream come true and Koko had the opportunity to be front and center. She left the event before it was over and she and Horace was talking about their night in her suite.

"Girl, yo' business page is on ten!" he said, going through all the new comments about the piece she made for Stephan. "The news segment put you on the map with the outside world. Koko! Taraji said something too!"

"What?"

"You heard me," Horace said looking up briefly. "This is what she said. *Koko knows how to bring realistic things to life with a brick of chocolate. I admire her work and I will be reaching out to the best so she can whip something up for me. I'll be talking to you soon, Miss ma'am."*

"Oh my God! I haven't even added the photo to my social media page yet. This is unbelievable!"

"Believe it, boo. You deserve everything coming your way. I told you long ago you were going to be a household name."

"You sure did. Thank you for believing in me, Horace."

"Thank me by believing in yourself from now on. It feels good to hear everyone else praise you, but you have to praise yourself just as much. You are a rare breed, Koko. It's only up from here and I'll be there every step of the way."

Instead of thanking him again, Koko got up and hugged him. Tears fell from her eyes and hit his shoulder. Horace pushed her back a bit with a frown on his face.

"Why are you crying?"

"I don't know," she sobbed.

"That alcohol is taking you through it, friend." Horace laughed. "Why the hell you drink all that champagne when you can't hang? I was about to say let's pop this tequila open but you've had enough."

"Nooooo, we can continue to celebrate. I just had a moment."

Koko wiped her face and walked away to get the bottle along with two glasses. She sat down beside him and poured both of their poison. The thought of Kazimir took over her mind shaking her head. Horace watched her smile in amazement. His friend was just crying her heart out now she seemed happy.

"Koko, what has you smiling all of a sudden?"

"Did you see how that woman tried to throw her being married to Kazimir at me?"

"I wanted to talk about that, but it wasn't the time nor the place. We are alone now and its free game," Horace said shifting his body around on the sofa to get comfortable.

147

"Kazimir is one fine muthafucka and I saw how he was whispering sweet nothings in your ear. One would've thought y'all was a couple the way he had you grinning from ear to ear."

"It wasn't even like that. Kazimir was just reassuring me that I would be okay. I was nervous as hell to go up on the stage. There was nothing intimate about the interaction."

Koko left out what Kazimir said to her because she didn't take him seriously. Especially, since she knew he had a wife. But she couldn't lie and say he didn't make her feel special at the time. He got the job done and made sure she stood with her head high. She appreciated the fact that he stood next to her.

"Shid, could've fooled me. That man has the hots for you, Koko. He's an upgrade from Cyrus nasty dick ass."

"He's also married. Don't leave that part out of the equation," she said rolling her eyes. "Kazimir is a man who's taking care of his business from what I can see. We won't mention the man who shall not be named in my presence. I've already had to cuss his ass out for questioning me with his bullshit."

"When was this?"

"While I was in the bathroom before we left the event. He texted talking about he saw me with the nigga from the club and he bet not be with me at this late hour. The negro also said don't make him hit the road. I called his ass and went clean the fuck off on him. Lil stupid dude better mind his damn business before I hurt his feelings."

"Wait, Kazimir was the man that got you off Jackie's ass in the club?"

Koko nodded.

"Well hell, he could've carried me to the end of the world. He fine as hell with his Lance Gross looking ass."

"See! I thought the same thing when I first laid eyes on him. Kazimir is good on the eyes. But I just have to remember he is married."

"Koko, he don't love that woman. He may be married by law, but he damn sure ain't happy."

"I know how it feels to be cheated on, Horace. I would never deal with another woman's man knowing he will go back home to her. I'm not into breaking up any home. If there will be any type of relationship between me and Mr. St. Claire, it will be business only."

Horace raised his glass to his lips then looked at Koko. "If you say so, boss. I'll put money on it that he is going to come for you on a whole other level. I've never been wrong and I'll put life savings on the table."

"Whatever."

As Koko sat back sipping her drink, her phone rang on the table. She reached for it and groaned when she saw who was calling. It had been months since she had heard from her mother and Koko already had a clue where the conversation was about to head before she even accepted the call. If Cyrus saw her on the news, then she knew her mother saw the segment as well. Koko hit the button to answer the call and placed it on speaker.

"Hello," she said dryly.

"Kameeko, when were you going to tell me you were in Chicgao?"

"I didn't think I had to. I mean, I haven't heard from you in how long? Now that you've seen me on the news you want to know my every move. Is that how parenting works?"

"Meeko, I will find you and beat your ass! I'm still your mama. Without me you wouldn't even be in the position you are in life. You came from my ovaries. My eggs took part in creating your ungrateful ass. Therefore, you owe me a fraction of what you have earned."

Koko chuckled openly at her mother. She couldn't believe what she said at first, but then again, she had to remember who the woman was on the other end of the phone. Her mother always felt belittling her daughter was the answer to getting her way. When Koko was younger, she thought never going against Nadine and showing unconditional love would eventually cause her mother to love her in return. Nope, it didn't happen. The more successful Koko became, the more Nadine loved receiving the money that came along with it. Hell, Koko wasn't even rich at the time. She just made lots of money. Her mother didn't give a damn long as she got her share of blue faces. The moment Koko said enough was enough, all the calls came to a halt and the hatred grew. Now Koko owed her.

"Nadine—"

"I'm your mother! Respect me as such, little girl. Don't ever address me by my first name!"

Koko looked up at Horace listening in horror. He couldn't believe the disrespect coming from Koko's mama. Opening his mouth to speak, his friend shook her head to keep him quiet, and closed her eyes for a second.

"You may have birthed me, and brought me into this world, but you will forever be Nadine to me for the rest of your natural life. You have to give respect to receive it. The name I've made for myself was my doing. My craft is just that; mine. I did everything I've accomplished on my own. It was me who worked my ass off at Bank of America to pay for school because you refused to fill out the financial aid forms. When I didn't know any better, I gave you so much money and I didn't get one thank you in return. So, to think I would do something like that a second time, you are out of your mind!"

"You ugly—"

"Nope. You won't do that either. See, being away from you all of these years allowed me to see how beautiful I actually am. That shit won't work this time. Nadine, you can call me whatever the fuck you want but that shit doesn't hurt me one iota. In your mind I'm uglier than a muthafucka and in mine, I'm a Nubian Queen. I will have children one day and I have to thank you for showing me how a mother shouldn't be toward her kids. My children will be loved.

That's something I truly want to thank you for because you were a shitty parent to me." Koko paused for a second before giving Nadine a chance to say anything else vial.

"On that note, I'm not giving you a dime of my money because I don't owe you shit! Whatever jam you're in, that's on you. I haven't heard from you nor your kids in God knows how long. I've been through so much in the last four years and I had to deal with that shit by myself. I didn't have anyone in my life to help me out of the rut I was in. Have that same energy and get yourself out of whatever situation you're facing. Or ask one of the kids you think so highly of. Oh, you can't because they don't have shit either. I would greatly appreciate if you wouldn't dial my number again after tonight."

"Kameeko, hear me out, baby. I never meant to hurt you. The things I've said to you is a way of me copping with the fact that you are successful just like your daddy and he too turned his back on me once he started making money."

"See, that's a lame ass excuse you just came up with. I've been the brute of all your mistreatment since I was a young girl. This didn't just start," Koko chuckled. "What my daddy did to you should have never been the reason you treated me like an orphan. Stop while you're ahead. Please. I'm standing on what I said before, I don't have anything else for you financially."

"Kameeko, I'm sorry."

"I know you are, but the answer is still no. Goodnight, Nadine."

Koko ended the call because she was on the verge of revealing how strong she was not when it came to her mother. It took everything in her not to breakdown while on the phone. Soon as she placed the phone on the table, Koko could no longer hold in her tears. She broke. Horace embraced his friend because he knew firsthand how hard it was to stand up to a member of the family. He was once in

Koko's shoes and it took a very long time for him to stand comfortably in his truth.

"Come on, boo. You said what you had to say and that's the end of it. No disrespect, but your mama is a piece of shit. You are beautiful, extremely talented, and you're beyond good enough. Don't ever allow anyone's words make you cry like this. I don't care if it was your mama. She is mad at your father and jealous of you. Keep doing what you're doing because it's working for you."

"She's been demeaning the hell out of me all my life. I'm tired, Horace," Koko cried. "She sees me on T.V. and think that's her payday. I'm no longer feeling sorry for her."

"You don't have to do that anymore. Stand your ground. She has the audacity to call you ugly and think that shit is going to give her access to your hard-earned money. Wipe your face, Koko. Make this the last time you shed a tear about this bullshit."

There was a knock on the door and Koko sat up wiping her eyes. She wondered who could be at her hotel suite at that time of the night. Nobody knew where she was staying. Horace stood to answer the door because Koko didn't move an inch. He looked through the peephole and turned to glance back at his friend. Instead of telling her who was on the other side, Horace opened the door with a smile. Koko needed to get all the bullshit from her mother and Cyrus off her mind. When Horace stepped to the side, Koko stood to her feet.

"Kazimir, what are you doing here?" she asked. "How did you know where I was?"

Kaz walked further into the room carrying a small bag. Horace cleared his throat as he held the door open. Koko knew what he was about to do, and she pled with her eyes.

"I'm about to go to my room. Hit my line if you need me, or just come over." He winked.

"You don't have to leave. I don't believe Mr. St. Claire will be here too long. He has a wife to get home to."

Kaz turned to Horace. "I got her from here, brah. She'll be alright."

"I know she's in good hands. Goodnight, boo. Do something that I'd do." He smirked as he left.

"Horace!"

Koko yelled after her friend, but it was in vain because Horace was long gone. Kazimir latched the door for whatever reason and made his way across the room to Koko. Handing her the bag, she took it, but her eyes was on the man standing in front of her. Kaz didn't answer her question, and she was waiting patiently. The way he studied her face was kind of making Koko uncomfortable.

"To answer your initial question, Stephan gave me the information on what hotel you were in. He also gave me the room number. I wanted to apologize for Nicolette's actions tonight and to give an explanation as to why she came off the way she did."

"You don't owe me an explanation, Kazimir. I was over that once she left the event. Honestly, it was quite funny and entertaining. You should give her more attention. Maybe her insecurities will go away." Koko sat down examining the bag Kazimir had given her. When she saw the golden wrapper, she shrieked loudly. "Oh my God! No, you didn't bring me my favorite caramel! Thank you so much. You just made my night."

Kazimir watched as Koko hurriedly unwrapped a piece of the candy then popped it in her mouth. He still wanted to address the redness of her eyes and why she was crying. Kazimir wanted to be the man to keep her smiling for the rest of her days. The nigga she was with didn't know the type of gem he had in her. Kazimir had plans to level her up to the status of her talent; if she allowed him to do so. He had to tell her about his situation in order for her to understand.

"I see you're smiling now, but why were you in here crying?" Koko held her head down and he lifted it back up with his finger. "What did I tell you about fixing yo' crown?

When I'm talking to you, or anybody for that matter, look them muthafuckas in their face. Now, talk to me, ma. What happened?"

Koko unwrapped another piece of candy and popped it in her mouth. She thought about how much she wanted to reveal because Koko hated putting too many people in her business. Kazimir waited while she sat quietly. Koko was taking too long so he figured he would give her a little push to talk.

"I got all day, Koko. I'm not leaving until I know the who, what, when, and why of your sadness."

"Okay. I received a call from my mother after she saw me on the news. She only called because she wants money and I'm not giving her any. I moved away because my mother has it in her mind that I'm supposed to take care of her and my siblings. Since I was making treats out of her kitchen, she saw what type of money I was bringing in. Soon as I won the cash prize on the cooking show, her hand was always out."

The sadness in Koko's eyes returned and Kaz didn't like it one bit. He sat waiting for her to continue. However long it took, he would be there to hear her out.

"When I was younger, she would call me every name in the book except the one she had given me at birth. I always felt like an outsider but I did whatever to make her happy but nothing ever did. I helped her put my sister through school. Took care of my other sister Daniyah and her three kids, and even my brother Donald. I'm not doing that shit anymore because they aren't doing anything for themselves. Now, she wants to be sorry because I told her ass no."

A tear fell from Koko's eye, but she swiped it away quickly. Kaz felt sorry for her, but she was on the right path of standing up for herself. He sat down beside her, refraining himself from gathering her in his arms. Instead, Kaz figured he would tell her the truth about what took place when money was involved.

154

EMBRACING THE LOVE OF A BOSS | MEESHA

"Koko, with success comes greed. Family is the first to hold their hands out for money. It's up to you if you're going to lend a helping hand. From what you have told me, you did all you needed to do before you became the entrepreneur you are today. The one thing you can't do is allow anybody to drain you of your fortune before its established. Take care of yourself and your business first and foremost. Anything outside of that is irrelevant."

As she listened to every word, Koko nodded. She knew what had to be done at that point, and that was to leave her mother and siblings right where they were; on the outside looking in. They wouldn't do anything except bring her down. Koko's mission was to rise, not fall. She made up her mind to leave her past in the past and work on elevating her business. Kazimir's voice brought her out of her thoughts.

"When I told you I would be there with you every step of the way, Koko, I meant what I said."

"Kazimir, you can't be there for me. Hell, you should be home with your wife right now. It's well after midnight and you're in another woman's hotel room. That's disrespectful in my eyes."

"You say I don't have to explain my situation, but I feel it's necessary that I do. All I want you to do is listen," Kaz said. "I'm only married to Nicolette on paper. We were married almost three years ago as a business deal between her father and my grandfather. It's an arranged marriage, Koko. I don't love her. Never have. For years, I've slept with numerous women just so I wouldn't have to sleep with Nicolette. Up until over a month ago, I would fuck a different woman whenever I got the urge. That hasn't been the case since I met you. It's been palm to dick with me thinking about you."

Koko didn't believe a word coming from his mouth, but it didn't prevent her from blushing after she heard his revelation. "Kazimir, you didn't know you were going to see me at Stephan's event. Stop lying about the reason you stopped sleeping with all of those women." She laughed. "On a serious tip though, why have you stayed in the marriage so long if it's not what you want? You can't move on with someone else if you're still married. And if I remember correctly, you have a child by this woman."

Kazimir ran his hand down his face. He stood and walked to the mini bar then came back with an empty glass and a bottle of Cognac. Taking his seat next to Koko, she tucked her feet under her butt as she watched him pour the liquor in the glass. Kazimir looked stressed discussing his personal life. He threw the alcohol back and poured another. He took a sip and placed the glass on the table.

"Nicolette and I don't have a child together. Alessia is the reason I was forced to marry her. Nicolette's father didn't want her to have a child out of wedlock. I'm not the biological father, Koko. Alessia is innocent in this shit, and I will forever be there for her. When I say I have never slept with her mother, that's the truth. We've been married damn near three years, and I haven't touched that woman. We are married on paper only."

"Why won't you get a divorce if you're not happy?" Koko asked.

"Nicolette's father is a very dangerous man. Not that he scares me, but I don't want to put my grandfather in harm's way. Santoro put up a lot of money to save the business. He refused to take a monetary payout and forced marriage instead. It's not like I don't have the money, I can pay the muthafucka to take his daughter back. He's not willing to do that. My peace has been disturbed far too long and I don't know how much more I can take. Especially, with Nicolette showing her ass in public like she did tonight."

"Why did she wait this long to start acting this way?"

"Nicolette has voiced a lot to me privately. Tonight was her first time doing it in a public setting. She is threatened now."

"Threatened by who?"

"You."

"Me?" Koko looked at him with a bewildered expression. "Why would she be threatened by me? I'm confused. I have nothing to do with what's going on in your marriage."

Kazimir looked deeply into her eyes. Koko was so beautiful to him, and he could no longer hide the way he felt for her. Even though he had only seen her twice in his lifetime, Kaz knew he needed her by his side. Koko was driven, determined, and had a future ahead of her. He also saw from the brief interactions between them, she needed someone to love her the way she deserved.

"You don't have anything to do with what I have going on, but Nicolette sees something you don't." Koko's eyebrow rose as she waited for him to finish his thought. "She has never seen me be so attentive to a woman before. She stood back watching me guide you through your nervousness and took it as me and you being together intimately."

"I hope you explained that we aren't on that level. The last thing I need is more drama in my life. You need to get out of your marriage and fast. I don't see any good coming from the situation if neither one of you are happy. What are you going to do when you finally find the woman you actually want to marry and have children with?"

"I'll cross that bridge when I get to it. Right now, I just want to make sure you and your business gets off to a good start. The next level of success can and will be stressful." Kaz picked up his glass and tossing the contents back. "I want to go further with my sponsorship. You don't have to answer now, but I'm going to lay it on the table anyway. What do you think about joining forces with St. Claire Candies? You can still do what you love, but with the backing of me. I will make sure you have a workspace to call your own, along with a full staff."

Koko was honored that Kazimir wanted to go an extra mile to help her, but she didn't think it was a wise decision to work in close proximities with him. Sitting beside him on the sofa was sending mixed signals to her honeypot. The scent of his cologne was an aphrodisiac by itself. As he spoke, she watched his lips move but didn't hear anything he said after the word staff.

"Did you hear me?" Kaz asked.

"Thank you for considering me to join your team, Kazimir. But I think I'm going to have to pass. I watched Fantasia in an interview, and she shared something her grandmother told her. She said, *you have a gift. Don't let nobody prostitute it.* I felt that with every fiber within me. If I come up with the ideas, build the clientele, and put in the work, I should be the one to bring in one hundred percent of the profits. I made a vow to myself when I first started my business; to never give anyone control over what I worked hard for."

"Believe me, I understand," Kaz said with a nod. "I don't want anything financially from you, Koko. All of your earnings would be yours to put in your bank account. My percentage will be zero. I'm trying to build you up; not break you down nor rip you off. The offer stands whenever you decide to take me up on what I presented."

Kaz felt good being able to talk to someone about what he's been going through. Koko was a nice listening ear, and he was comfortable being in her presence. He didn't want to leave but he knew he had to, or he would be labeled a creep when he touched her. The urge to pull Koko in for a kiss was high and it would be very inappropriate for him to do. Standing to his feet, Kaz stretched while looking over her body.

"It's late. I think I'm going to head out. Enjoy the remainder of your stay. I'll make sure to keep in touch," he said revealing one of her business cards.

"Kaz. I can see us becoming very good friends. My line is open so you can call whenever you like. Drive safely." Koko smiled. "Oh, thanks again for the caramels. I'll still have to get more because these will not last the next two days."

"Slow down on the sweets. You'll be up all night from a sugar rush."

They laughed as Koko popped a piece of candy into her mouth before getting up to walk Kaz to the door. When she got back to her suite after the event, Koko took a shower and changed into a pair of leggings and a tank top. Her ass was sculpted just right for Kaz's liking and he couldn't take his eyes off the way it jiggled with every step she took. She turned around swiftly, and he had to divert his eyes just as fast.

"Well," Kaz said clearing his throat. "It was good seeing you again. Thanks for being a listening ear."

"Likewise. I guess both of us had to get some things off our chests tonight. Think about what I said. It may seem like your marriage isn't all it's cracked up to be but try to go a little easier on the wife's feelings. Your life could be a lot peaceful."

"The rules of fair play do not apply in love and war. There isn't any love in this marriage, Koko. But we are always at war. I have to do what is best for me and I want happiness at this point. I'm going to do everything in my power to get it too."

Kaz stepped forward, wrapping his arms around her waist. The way he hugged her caused Koko to damn near melt into his body. He was so tall that her head rested on his chiseled abs instead of his chest. She could feel the bulge in his pants and his ass was packing a mean pistol. Koko stepped back to put space between them.

"Goodnight, Kameeko. I need you to get some sleep. No phone, T.V.; none of that. Relax. Can you do that for me?"

"I hear you. Goodnight, Mr. St. Claire."

"What I tell you to call me, shorty? Don't worry about it. You will be calling me Kaz in no time," he said, bending down to kiss her forehead. "Get some rest." Kaz flipped the latch and showed himself out of the suite.

Soon as the door closed behind him, she leaned against it and sighed deeply. The only thing that stood in the way of her climbing into Kaz's lap was the fact of him being legally married. If he was single, he could've gotten deep into the tight walls of her essence. She was glad they wouldn't cross paths again because she wasn't sure she would be able to resist him a third time.

Chapter 11

Nicolette stretched as she prepared herself to get up to start her day. Smiling, she turned over to snuggle beside her husband, but he wasn't there. The dream she had was just that; a dream. She should've known he hadn't sexed her like no man had ever done because he had never even touched her in an intimate manner. The smile turned into a frown quickly as she flung the sheet from her body. Walking across the huge master bedroom, Nicollette entered the bathroom to take care of her hygiene.

She stepped into the bedroom a half hour later then went into her closet to grab an outfit for the day. Nicolette wasn't the type of woman to dress down. That day, she decided to put on a pair of white capris, a pink t-shirt, and a pair of pink Nikes she had never worn. Kazimir bought her the shoes one day over a year prior. Nicolette felt cheap in the outfit and wanted to change immediately. The knock on the door was the reason she didn't.

"What is it, Marisol?" Once she saw who was on the other side of the door.

"Mrs. St. Claire, Alessia is very distraught. She's been crying uncontrollably all morning. I don't know what could be wrong. Please come with me to check on her."

"I will not come with you. Take her to her father," Nicolette stated irritably. "I have things to do and dealing with Alessia isn't one of them."

"I'm sorry, but Mr. St. Claire isn't home."

"Well, she's your problem. Go do what you're paid to do. Be the fucking nanny!"

Nicolette slammed the door in Marisol's face just as her phone started ringing. She picked the device up from the nightstand and sighed when she saw her father's name on the display. She really didn't want to answer but there would've been consequences if she didn't. Pushing the icon to accept the call, Nicolette put on her happy face when she addressed him.

"Hey, father. How are you?"

"Cut the shit, Nicolette," he snarled in her ear. "What the hell is your husband doing in the streets?"

"What do you mean?"

"You went to the black-tie event for Renaissance Railroad last night, correct?"

At that moment, Nicolette knew exactly what her father was talking about. She couldn't admit to witnessing the way Kazimir acted with the woman who was getting all the praises in the building. Her father would've wanted to know why was she still breathing.

"Nicolette!"

"I'm here. I did go to the event, but I was late. Kazimir and I weren't on the best terms and I told him I wasn't going to attend. I decided to go at the last minute. When I arrived, nothing was going on. So, I don't have any idea what you're referring to."

It didn't take long for a video to be sent to her phone via text. Nicolette already knew what happened on the video, so she pretended to watch it. Her father wanted her and Kazimir's marriage to seem real as possible. Kazimir was making her look like a fool in public. Anthony wasn't going to let him live that shit down.

"Who is that woman?" Nicolette asked.

"A black bitch that's out to get your husband. How the hell did you allow him to roam alone?"

"I didn't allow him to do anything. Kazimir is a grown man that does what he wants, when he wants." Nicolette tried her best to keep her voice down.

Yelling at her father was a form of disrespect and she didn't want to open that can of worms with him. Nicolette had been keeping everything she and her husband were going through from her father. It was about time she let him in on how miserable she was in the marriage.

"Kazimir doesn't want me as his wife. For the duration of this marriage, he hasn't touched me once. Not a hug, a kiss, nothing. All I've received from him is material things I can buy on my own. When I said I do during my fairytale wedding, my plan was to live happily ever after with my knight in shining armor. It's been the total opposite. All of Kazimir's love is directed towards Alessia. My husband gets his sexual satisfaction on the other side of the door. Never with me."

Anthony paced in his home office, fuming with anger. When he volunteered to help Paxton save his business, the first thought was to tax him on the dollar. Once Nicolette revealed she was pregnant and the father of her child had forced himself on her, Anthony knew she couldn't be a mother out of wedlock. Paxton talked highly of his grandson whenever they sat down to talk business and Anthony came up with a way for Paxton to repay his debt. Unbeknownst to Kazimir, there wasn't a contract which bound him to stay with Nicolette. Truthfully speaking he could've left after Alessia was born. It was too late for that shit now because he was going to honor the vows he recited at the altar.

"Why am I hearing about this mistreatment years later? I know he doesn't care for me because he didn't have a say so in who he married, but he is supposed to treat you with the utmost respect at all times. Put his ass on the phone now!"

"He's not here. Kazimir didn't come home last night."

"The son of a bitch stayed out with that homewrecking bitch! He is skating on thin ice, and I will have a few choice words for him. He is your husband! There is no getting out of the marriage. He vowed to love you 'til death and that's the only way he would leave. In a fucking body bag."

"Please don't do anything to harm him. Without her father, Alessia would be heartbroken. I may not be happy with how things are going, but he means the world to her."

"He's not her father! Did he sign the birth certificate while he's lollygagging around with another woman?"

"He's the only father she knows! You killed her biological daddy," Nicolette sobbed.

"Why did I kill the bastard? He violated you in the worst way and I thought I told you not to mention what I'd done. I need you to act like your maiden name is Santoro! Being a St. Claire has made you soft. We don't cry about shit! I don't give a fuck how much it hurts. The rules have not changed, Nicolette. I need you to toughen up. Did he sign the birth certificate?" he asked again.

"No. He said he doesn't need to sign it in order to be her father. The only way he will sign is if I was on my deathbed. His words, not mine."

"Okay. I definitely need to talk to his ass. Don't be in that house crying. I got it from here. How's my granddaughter?"

"She's fine. I'm about to go check on her now. Kazimir isn't here and Alessia is having a tantrum about it."

"Well, you are her mother. Go take her off Marisol's hands. You can deal with her better than the help. I'll talk to you later."

Anthony ended the call without saying he loved her. That told her Anthony was mad because of what Kazimir was doing. Nicolette rolled her eyes because nobody understood why she only dealt with her daughter in front of others. Alessia was with Nicolette majority of the time and with the nanny the remainder. But the only person she called out for was *daddy*. Kazimir was barely home but he was the person she looked forward to seeing every day. Thinking about it enraged her.

Nicolette left the room following the cries of her two-year-old daughter. When she entered the nursery, Alessia was throwing a tantrum in the arms of Marisol. Her face was beet read and she was sweating as if she had just run a marathon. Trying her best to consol the toddler, Marisol whispered something in her ear. Alessia wasn't trying to hear none of it.

"Nooooooo! Daddy!"

Stepping into the room, Nicolette roughly snatched her daughter up. "Cut it out! You are doing too much right now." She scolded. "Marisol, I have it from here. I'll dress her this morning. Did she have breakfast yet?"

"No, ma'am. She's been this way since she realized Mr. St. Claire wasn't home."

"Well, the fiasco ends now. We'll be down in a few. You can leave now." Nicolette dismissed her with a wave of her hand. Hesitating to leave the little girl in her mother's presence alone, Marisol didn't budge. "Go cook breakfast! I don't need you to watch me calm my child down," Nicolette sneered.

Rushing out of the room, Marisol made her way downstairs as she shook with fear. She had witnessed Nicolette mistreat Alessia on several occasions. It hadn't turned physical, but it would be a matter of time before it got to that point. The sound of the alarm beeping indicated someone had entered the residence. It could only be one person and Marisol was happy he had shown up. Kazimir rounded the corner just as she stepped off the last stair.

"Good morning, Marisol. How are you?"

"I'm fine, Mr. St. Claire. Alessia is another story. She has been crying for you. It seems as if you will be the only person to calm her heart."

"How long has this gone on today?" he asked.

"A few hours. Mrs. St. Claire is with her now."

Marisol bit into her bottom lip and wrung her hands nervously. She looked away but Kazimir read her body

165

language very well. Something was off and she was afraid to speak on it. Marisol excused herself to the kitchen and he followed.

"What's going on?"

Marisol busied herself to prepare breakfast without answering.

"Stop for a second. Did something happen that I should know about?"

"I need my job here, Mr. St. Claire. I'm going to do what I was paid to do and that's make sure Alessia is okay at all times."

Kazimir didn't like the way she expressed what she said and felt his adrenaline starting to rise. There was more behind Marisols statement, he was sure. What he wasn't going to do was leave it at that. "Marisol, talk to me. Your job is forever secure. Do not keep secrets from me," Kazimir said calmly. "Whatever is going on, I need to know so I can get to the bottom of it."

Marisol turned and eyed the doorway before she put the spoon she was holding onto the counter. Glancing down at her feet, Kazimir walked over, lifting her head with his finger. She was very shifty and he didn't like it. He'd always treated his workers like family and didn't know what could be so bad that Marisol felt she couldn't talk about it with him. If there was something wrong, he wanted to know about it.

"I'm waiting. What you say will stay between us. When the time presents itself, I will be sure to keep your name out of the mix when I handled the problem."

"Alessia misses you. She throws tantrums when you're not around, Mr. St. Claire. I try my best to calm her before going to Mrs. St. Claire, but it doesn't work all the time." She paused. "I'm worried her mother will do something to harm her. Again, I'm not trying to cause any trouble. But Alessia is not in good hands when she's not with me. Mrs.

St. Claire sent me away and I think you should go upstairs and check on the baby."

"Is she harming Alessia?" Kazimir was dreading her response and braced himself.

"Not that I know of. I make sure to examine her body daily. It's the way she talks to her that bothers me. I mean, Alessia is two; she's still a baby and she's being cursed out like an adult for wanting her father. That's not right. Being called a bitch from your own mother could be detrimental to her mental state further in life. Yelling for her to shut up because she's crying doesn't help either."

Kaz was pissed as he listened to some of the things Nicolette was subjecting Alessia to. The anger she had towards him had nothing to do with Alessia. She knew the little girl was his heart and he had to make it his business to be there for her because her mother was being a piece of shit. If anything happened to Alessia by the hands of Nicolette, Kaz wouldn't hesitate to make her pay in blood.

"Thank you so much for telling me. I think making Alessia's favorite blueberry Minnie Mouse pancakes will make her happy. I'll have her down shortly."

"You and I are on the same page. I was already starting to prepare those." Marisol smiled. "Mr. St. Claire, thank you for not being mad at me. I will bring all of my concerns about Alessia to you immediately. I've thought about calling but your wife told me to never contact you when you're not home."

"Negative. You have my number; you don't have to go through her to call me. Far as you informing me about what's going on around here, that won't be necessary either. In due time, I would be able to see everything even when I'm not here. I'm heading upstairs now. See you in a bit."

Kaz left out of the kitchen and climbed the stairs. He immediately heard Alessia crying from her bedroom. As he neared the door, she cried out for him. Kaz's heart felt as if someone squeezed it because he wondered how often she'd become distraught like that. It was Nicolette's rebuttal to her crying that caused him to stop in his tracks for a brief moment.

"He's not here and that's not your daddy! Now, I've told you to shut the fuck up and allow me to comb your hair!"

When he stepped into the doorway, he saw Alessia squirming on her mother's lap. Nicolette was trying to comb her hair. That didn't matter because how she was talking to her was the problem.

"Bitch, be still!"

"Nicolette, I will break your muthafuckin' neck," Kaz sneered.

"Daddy!"

He took Alessia from her mother while glaring at her. "Why are you in here screaming, cursing, and calling her out of her name? She's a baby!"

"Do you hear her crying now? She has been hooping and hollering all morning. You come in and now she's quiet as a church mouse."

"What do that have to do with the way you've been talking to her? This wasn't the first time because you seem quite comfortable with the way you communicate with her. Instead of cursing at her, you should be teaching her numbers, ABCs, and colors."

"How dare you tell me what I should be doing! You're never here to assist with her! On top of that, I don't get a choice of when I want to play mama! I'm mama twenty-four seven!"

"Correction, you're her mother maybe two hours out of the day. Marisol is her nanny and is more of a mother than you are. You know what, I'm not about to carry on like this in front of her. We'll talk about this later. Give me the comb and brush. I'll finish her hair."

Nicolete tossed the items onto the bed and walked toward the door. She turned back around with pure hate in her eyes as she watched Kazimir brush Alessia's hair into a ponytail.

The fact that she sat there without making a peep pissed Nicolette off.

"While you're in the mood to be daddy, I hope you don't have plans for the day. Alessia will be with you because I'm going out to enjoy the rest of my day. Don't wait up."

"I have no problem with that. Have fun," Kaz said without looking up from the task at hand. "You're hanging with me today, baby girl. That's cool with you?"

"Yes, daddy. Ice cream?"

"Anything you want, I got you."

Nicolette left the room in a huff. She went into the bedroom grabbing her purse and car keys before leaving the house completely. Once she got into her Porche, Nicolette circled around the driveway and out of the gate. Kazimir was going to see what it was like to be a full-time parent because she wasn't going back to the house until she was ready.

***

After Alessia ate, she and Kaz had a fun day of playing tea party then watched a little bit of Cocomelon. That show alone had him thinking about the chocolate beauty he left the night before. As he sat smiling at the little girl he loved beyond measures, Kaz took his phone from his pocket and sent Koko a text.

(773)555-0098: Hey, I wanted to know if you wanted to meet me for ice cream if you're not busy.

Koko: Um, who is this?

(773) 555-0098: It's your future. You just don't know it yet. How many caramels do you have left?

Koko: LOL Kazimir! How are you? Ice cream? You don't look like an ice cream type of guy. To answer your question though, Horace and I were going to head over to Navy Pier to check out the Illuminarium, Wild: A Safari Experience. If you don't mind me bringing a date, we can meet you afterward.

(773) 555-0098: That's fine because I'm bringing someone along with me as well. It can be a double date.

Koko hoped like hell he didn't bring his wife along with him. After the way she put on at the event, Koko didn't know if she could be in the woman's presence. She dialed Horace's phone to tell him about their unexpected plan change. Of course, he was all for meeting up with Kazimir because he wanted Koko to get to know the man.

Kaz had some time to waste because it would take thirty minutes to get to the city. Give or take traffic. Koko would be at Navy Pier for about an hour so that gave him enough lead way to get there. Marisol was redoing Alessia's hair because the ponytail Kaz had done wasn't going to be a good look for outside. He noticed she was all smiles since Nicolette had left the house. Something was going on behind closed doors and he was going to use that day to get a head start on finding out. Picking up his phone, Kaz made a call to his good friend Eduardo.

"Kaz, how's it going?"

"Everything is good. I need you to come do a job for me, if you're not busy of course."

"It's Saturday and I have nothing to do at this moment. What do you need?"

Kaz walked onto the back patio closing the door behind him. "I need a few cameras installed inside the house. Today will be the best time because Nicolette won't be back for a while. Is it possible?"

"You're in luck because I just restocked equipment yesterday. I have some high-tech shit that's yours if you want it. I can be there in the next twenty minutes."

"Let's do it. I'll be here waiting."

Kaz made a call to Koko so he could push back the time for them to meet up. The call went into voicemail so he waited for the beep to leave a message. "Koko, I'm going to have to meet up with you later. I have to get some things done at the house before I can leave out. Hopefully, I'll see you soon."

Walking back inside, Kaz was met by a squealing Alessia. "My hair," she said pulling at her ponytails.

"You are beautiful, baby."

"Ice cream?"

"We're going soon. Daddy has some work to do first. Let's go back and watch more T.V. Or maybe I can call mommy to take you."

"No mommy! Me want go wit' you!"

Alessia hugged his neck tightly so he wasn't able to put her down. Instead, Kaz went into the living room and sat on the sofa. He wanted to question her but thought against it. Soon enough Kaz would be able to see with his own eyes what went on behind his back. Alessia was sleeping before the third song played and he laid her down when the doorbell rang. Eduardo showed up sooner than expected.

"Thanks for coming on such short notice. I'll pay you double," Kaz said as he ushered his friend inside.

"You don't have to pay me at all because I know this has a lot to do with Nicolette's ass. I didn't want to say anything over the phone because I wanted to see your reaction face to face. Now, tell me what's going on while I work. Where do you want these cameras? I have six of them."

Kaz had audio monitors throughout the home so Alessia could be heard when she cried out. Now he would be able to have eyes on her and everything else every minute of the day. He walked through showing Eduardo where to place the devices as he filled him in on what he thought Nicolette was doing. He was able to place five of them in different areas then put one in the cable box in Alessia's room. Eduardo instructed him to download the app so he would be able to see the footage live from his phone. Looking at his watch, he noticed it was a little after twelve. Koko still hadn't responded to his voicemail.

"Thank you again, Ed. You always come through."

"Kaz, if it wasn't for you, I wouldn't have a business to call my own. To be truthful, I'm in debt with you."

"Nah, you not. If I was looking for that investment money back, believe me when I tell you, I'd have it. Keep doing what you do, man. I want to see you rise to the top."

"I appreciate that man. If you need anything else, don't hesitate to call," Eduardo said opening the door to leave.

"Will do. Stay safe out there."

His phone vibrated in his pocket, and he pulled it out and smiled when he saw Chocolate Drop on the screen. Koko was calling. As he closed the door, he answered.

"Hello, Kameeko."

"Kazimir, I'm sorry. I just listened to your voicemail. Are you still conducting business?"

"Actually, I just finished. I can be on my way now, but it will take about thirty to forty minutes. Is that okay?"

"That's fine. Where do you want to meet? Or do you want to just come to the hotel?"

Koko's question caused his meat to harden in his pants. Asking him if he wanted to come to the place she was laying her head during her stay meant something totally different to Kaz. Shaking the thought from his head, he smiled before answering.

"No, I'll meet you at Cold Stone on Ohio. Wait for my call then you can be on your way."

"Sounds like a plan. Drive safely."

Ending the call, Kaz walked to the sofa to wake Alessia. She was sleeping soundly but he promised her ice cream and he was going to keep his word. It took a few minutes to get her to wake up. When she finally opened her eyes, Kaz kissed her cheeks making her laugh.

"Okay, are you ready to go get ice cream?"

"Yessssss, daddy!" she squealed climbing from the sofa.

Alessia ran to the door and that was Kaz's cue to grab his keys. He told Marisol she could leave for the day because Alessia was going to spend time with him. She was happy about that and ecstatic when Kaz said she would get her pay for the day as well. They all left the house together and just as he was buckling Alessia in her car seat, Nicolette drove up. She barely put the car in park when she jumped out on bullshit.

"Where are you taking my baby?" Nicolette yelled.

"We're going for ice cream."

"I'm going too."

"No, you're not. You were supposed to be out enjoying yourself. I told you Alessia would spend the rest of the day with me."

"Well, I'm here now and I'm going with you guys."

Kaz finished securing Alessia in the seat then closed the door. Walking around the car, he opened the driver's door and hit the key fob to activate the locks. Just as he thought, Nicolette pulled the handle to get inside. Kaz ignored her actions and started the engine. He backed out, avoiding her vehicle and drove away from the house. His phone started ringing immediately, but when he saw it was Nicolette, he didn't answer. She wasn't about to ruin his day out. Little did Kaz know, he woke up a monster.

Chapter 12

Sitting inside the ice cream shop, Koko and Horace talked about the event they had seen. She really enjoyed herself and had never been to anything like that when living in the city. Horace was still talking about meeting a thug on O'Block and Koko was over his shit. He just didn't know those thugs would eat him alive and spit him on the pavement. He was in a room full of money makers and all he could think about was hood niggas.

"Horace, why didn't you get the numbers of the men who were on your gaydar at Stephan's event?"

"Who's to say I didn't? They are the type you get to know so they won't think you're out for their hard-earned cash. Now, the thugs, as you call them, are the ones I want to pop this bussy for. Girl, you been out the loop entirely too long. I'm gonna need you to get with the program. There are levels to this shit."

Koko couldn't do anything but laugh at her friend because he was so serious about the ratchet analogy he spoke of. The things she had gone through with Cyrus would've turned the average female's heart cold as ice. Not Koko. She was still going to find the man who would love her for the woman she was. There was a man out there that would see her worth and cater to her as the love of her life. Another female was not going to be on his radar. Koko would be the only woman he would ever see.

Glancing out of the window, Koko took in a glimpse of a man holding a little girl's hand as they walked toward the entrance. She could only see a side view of the pair and didn't think anything of it. She looked down at her watch and it had been close to an hour since she'd hear from Kazimir. Hopefully, everything was okay because he didn't text when he was close.

"Daddy, pick up."

The sound of the little girl's voice tugged at Koko's heart strings because she longed to be a mother someday. She wanted to turn around to see how the dad interacted with his daughter but was afraid she would openly cry. The moment took her mind back to Cyrus' betrayal causing her to shake the thought away. Koko realized she had dodged a bullet when she removed herself from the relationship that wasn't meant to be. She did the right thing by setting Cyrus free to do what he wanted, and she was for sure going to do what was needed for herself.

The smile on Horace's face caused Koko to turn in the direction of his gaze. Kaz walked toward their table hand in hand with a little girl that didn't resemble him in no way. She was so pretty with her two pigtails and babydoll like eyes. He on the other hand looked good enough to eat. His swag was top tier as he moved along in a pair of black jeans, a white polo shirt which showcased his muscular build, and a pair of black and white sneakers. For Kaz to be a successful businessman, he sure didn't dress like one. Koko wasn't mad at him because nowadays people didn't need to know one had money. It was a magnet for the stickup kids.

"Hey! You're looking good," Koko said standing to give him a hug. "Who is this little cutie?"

"Thank you. You're looking really good yourself." Kaz held on to her longer than expected while still holding on to Alessia's hand. Koko's wore the scent he loved radiating from her skin.

"Off my daddy!" Alessia shrieked while pushing Koko away.

Kaz looked down at her with a frown. He opened his mouth to scold her but Koko's touch stopped him. Sitting down in the chair so she was almost at eye level with the child, Koko introduced herself.

"Hello, I'm Koko. What's your name?" she asked sweetly. Alessia buried her face into Kaz's leg without uttering a word. "Maybe we can start over fresh after we get ice cream. What do you think?"

"Ice cream?" she repeatedly looked up at Kaz. "I want Chocalak ice cream. Can I, daddy?"

Kaz nodded as Koko stood. She reached out to take Alessia's hand, but she refused to let go of her daddy's. Horace chuckled as he got up to decide what flavor ice cream he wanted. As they walked to the counter, Koko officially introduced the two. Of course, Horace had to be his messy self by trying to play matchmaker.

"So, Kazimir, I need you to take my girl on a date."

"Horace!" Koko sneered smacking his arm. "Why would you say something like that to this man while he has his daughter with him? On top of that, he's happily married."

"I'm working on it, man. She knows my situation, but it seems she's ignoring it. Patience is a virtue." He smirked. "One thing I won't do is rush her. I have some things I need to get under control on my end before approaching her in that manner. Koko is definitely on my radar."

"Kameeko needs a man to love her the right way. I believe you could be just what she needs in her life."

"Y'all are going to have a conversation about what I need as if I'm not standing right here?"

"I'm just trying to hook you up with an upstanding man."

"Well, drop it. For the last time, Kazimir is married. Can we order ice cream for the baby please?"

Turning away from them, Koko ordered for herself and Alessia then went back to the table. She watched as Kaz and

Horace ordered then talked quietly amongst themselves. Koko hoped like hell her friend wasn't conjuring up a plan to get her and Kazimir alone. She would have no problem cursing his ass out for interfering in her private life. There was no way she would ever date a married man, and that shit was final.

They came back to the table with the ice cream and Horace sat next to Koko to give the other side of the booth to Kaz and his daughter. Alessia kept peeking over the table and she could barely see over the top. Kaz got up to get a booster chair and the little girl followed his every move. Koko smiled at the little girl and tried to hold a conversation with her once again.

"How old are you, Alessia?" she asked even though she already knew the answer.

Holding up two fingers while still watching her father. Kaz was looking down at his phone as he hurried back to the booth. He propped the phone between his ear and shoulder and Koko got up to help him assist Alessia.

"Would you watch her for a moment? I have to take this call."

There was fire in Kaz's eyes causing Koko to stare at him intensely. Nodding, Kaz made his way out of the building. Alessia pouted then started tearing up as she strained her neck to see where her daddy had gone. Koko nudged Horace so she could get up. She joined Alessia on the other side pulling her ice cream to the other side of the table.

"Daddy will be right back. Do you like your ice cream?" Koko asked.

"I want daddy," she cried.

Koko thought of a way to stop her from crying. Cocomelon came to mind and she grabbed her phone and went straight to YouTube. Placing the phone in front of Alessia, she quieted down immediately while swaying to the music. Horace tried to hide his smile as he observed the interaction between her friend and her future stepdaughter.

At that point, Alessia dropped her guard including Koko into her world.

Outside, Kaz was fuming. Anthony was on his phone talking recklessly and it didn't sit well with the young entrepreneur. Other than being the owner of St. Claire's Candies, Santoro didn't know the type of man Kaz really was. The way he spoke to him about what was going on between him and Nicolette had Kaz enraged.

"Hold the fuck up! You calling me to express how I'm treating your daughter? I don't have to act like I love her ass! The agreement was for me to marry Nicolette. Nowhere in the agreement did I ever say I would treat her like my wife. I'm doing what I signed up to do and that's take care of Alessia. Anything outside of that is on y'all."

"No, you said I do along with everything that comes with the oath."

"Yous a muthafuckin' lie. Anthony, you arranged marriage for your daughter so she wouldn't be a mother out of wedlock. I married her to save my grandfather from losing his life. The offer still stands; I will pay whatever to get out of this shit. It will be three years in two month and I'm tired of this shit. The love of my life is out there, and your daughter is standing in the way of me finding her."

"Is this love of your life the woman I saw you with on the news?"

"It doesn't matter who the fuck it is. What it's not is Nicolette. Since day one I've never had any feelings for her. Nicolette and I have not consummated our fake marriage. That should tell you something right there. I don't see her in that manner, and it won't change with you talking shit."

"If you're not sleeping with Nikki, who are you sleeping with?"

"Like I told her, it's none of your business. Just know I get my share of pussy. I'm a man. Going without getting my dick wet is not an option."

"Did you say that shit to my daughter?" Santoro's yelled.

"I sure as fuck did. Why lie? Nicolette is a grown ass woman. It's your job to pacify her; not mine. If I'm not fucking her, she should know I'm fucking on somebody. I'm not about to go back and forth with you about this. I'm fine being Alessia's father, but I will no longer walk around worrying about being married to your daughter. Nicolette is tired of the arrangement and so am I. Tell her to file for the divorce and I will gladly sign off on that shit. I'm done."

Santoro was pissed as he paced in his office. Nicolette getting a divorce would be frowned upon and he couldn't have that. On top of it all, his finances weren't the same as they were three years prior. A few bad investments had him sitting in a bad position. Forcing Paxton's grandson to marry Nicolette was coming back to bite him in the ass. Karma was a bitch, and she was beating his ass along with his daughter.

"Kazimir, the only way you're getting out of this marriage is if you pay me six million dollars. That would ensure both Nicolette and Alessia is taken care of for years to come."

"You got me fucked up! The only money I was willing to give you was half a mil and that was because I deducted the rest from taking care of your daughter for years. Now, I'm not giving you shit! Muthafucka, who the fuck you think you're trying to strong-arm? I guess you thought you had a simp ass nigga, huh? I'm not my grandfather. I'll never have to depend on another nigga to keep my head above water."

"You may want to reconsider before making a final decision, Kazimir."

"Or what?" Kaz seethed. "I can already see where this is going. Keep your idle threats to yourself because once you voice that shit, I will make sure Nicolette is able to bury you in style. You better check my bloodline, muthafucka! While you're at it, make sure to talk to your daughter because if anything happens to Alessia in her care, she gon' have to deal with me. Get the fuck off my phone!"

Kaz hung up and Santoro looked down at his device before tossing it on the desk. He poured a glass of bourbon and downed it. As he looked out of the window, he grinned evilly. Kaz didn't want to play the game he started. There was no getting out. His life was going to go from sugar to shit in a matter of days and Santoro was going to bring him to his knees.

Kaz couldn't go back inside the way his adrenaline was racing. Anthony had made the choice for him to get out of the marriage with Nicolette. He didn't give a damn what her father had to say about it. Their time of playing house was over. While he was upset, Kaz decided to give Nicolette a heads up about what was going on. Pulling out his phone, he called her. The phone rang numerous times, but she didn't answer. That was good on her part because the things Kaz wanted to say would've for sure made her cry like a baby. The shit was going to be addressed the moment Nicolette was in his presence. Until then, he was going back to enjoy ice cream with his baby girl.

Soon as Kaz was about to head back into the ice cream shop, his phone rang. He retrieved it from his pocket and Steelo's name was on the display. Accepting the call, he was ready for whatever his partner was about to say.

"What's up?" Kaz asked.

"Aye, I just received a call from Lowkey. Shit in Minnesota ain't right. I don't how much you know, but there is a lot of paper coming up missing. That nigga don't know where it's going either. You said we were heading that way, but I think now is the time to get a jump on this shit."

"Lowkey isn't on his shit. We can roll out tomorrow. I'll have the jet fueled and ready to go because this nigga can't handle the job I put him in charge of. Why would he call you and not me?"

"You already know these muthafuckas think I'm the more sensible one out of the two of us. They done thought wrong because it's my fuckin' money they playing with too. Three hunnid thou is a lot of money to ignore."

"Three hundred thousand! Oh, hell nawl! That nigga made it seem as if only a pickup was short one time."

"Nah, this shit been ongoing for weeks according to Lowkey. He told you what he wanted to tell you to keep the peace. That's where he fucked up because we about to be on all they ass. I guess because you wear a suit and tie these niggas don't think you're a threat."

"None of these muthafuckas in the streets knows what the fuck I do during the day and I'm going to keep it that way. Only the niggas here in the Chi knows I'm the Plug. We gon' keep that shit on the low too. They done fucked around, now they gotta find out. I'll hit you up later to tell you what time we heading out. I have some shit to straighten out with Nicolette first."

"I hope you about to cut the strings from her ass. I've told you time again, I don't trust her or Santoro. They have been playing with you for years."

"That shit is coming to an end very soon. I'm gon' have problems out of Santoro and his damn daughter. The muthafucka gon' tell me he wants six mil to end the marriage."

"Man, he trippin'! He didn't even put up that much for Pax. Watch her ass because she could be just as treacherous as her daddy. I hope you covered your tracks well before going into this shit, Kaz. This shit feels like it was a setup from the start. If you want, I can have Phinx to look into Santoro's background."

"Nah, we have to figure out what's going on with the shit in Minnesota first. This mess with Santoro isn't fazing me at all. Everything will come to light in due time. It's pickup day."

"I'm already on it. My name is not Lowkey. I'm always on my shit and yours. No reminders needed over here. I've set up the team for the monthly delivery on the dock too. I should be getting the call sometime today about how everything turned out. We haven't had any problems, so shit should be straight."

"Aight, keep me posted."

"Bet."

Kaz was finally ready to go inside after pushing all the bullshit to the back. When he got to the table, Alessia was done with her ice cream and cleaned up. She and Koko were laughing and dancing in the seat. The smile on her face was one Kaz only see between he and her. They were singing the wheels on the bus song from Cocomelon. He walked over and joined in. Next thing he knew, everyone was having a grand time with his baby girl.

"Daddy!" Alessia giggled when she noticed him. "I have fun with Koko and uncle H."

"Yassssss, neicy pooh! Come give me an official hug because I got you from this day forward."

Aleesia tried her best to get out of the highchair. Koko stood to help her before placing her on the floor. She ran right into Horace's arms hugging his neck tightly. Kaz liked the way Horace embraced his daughter. The atmosphere changed soon as Koko glanced toward the entrance. The light dimmed from her eyes and the frown caused a few wrinkles along her mouthline. Kaz followed her gaze and didn't recognize the woman coming in their direction.

"Take Alessia outside," Kaz said, handing Horace the keys to his truck.

"What's going on?"

"I don't know. Just get her out of here."

Horace saw Koko's hands balled up into fists, causing him to glance up. The woman getting closer resembled his friend and he knew right away she was related in some type of way. Knowing the history Koko had with her family, yeah, it wasn't a place for his new niece to be. He hurried up and stood with Alessia making a beeline for the door. Kaz put his hand on Koko's waist but she shrugged him off.

"So, if it's not my lovely big sister." The woman smirked. "I want you to tell me no like you did mama. School is starting and you *will* buy my kids what they need."

Daniyah had Koko fucked up. What she said to her mother went for anybody associated with her money hungry ass. See, that was their problem always thinking she was going to come to their rescue with her funds. The shit was dead. If she had to beat the fuck out of her sister in public to prove her point; so be it. Kaz saw where the interacting was about to go and grabbed Koko by the arm leading her toward the door. Her resistance made him hold on firmer then bent down to whisper in her ear.

"This is not the place to do this. Let her ass talk. You said you were not helping anymore then stand on that shit," he snarled. "Putting on a show for these white muthafuckas is not the way to go, Koko. You have a reputation now. Any little thing can throw a monkey wrench in your plans. They will call the law faster than lightning, and you will be going to jail. I won't allow you to tarnish your name."

Koko understood what Kaz was saying and stopped putting up a fight to confront her ignorant ass sister. She walked out of Cold Stone with her head held high. Daniyah wanted to bring the ghetto downtown though. She talked more shit than a little bit as she followed them out of the door.

"Not only do you have the money to help your family out, but you got this rich nigga on your arm on top of it. So, when are you going to send me two thousand dollars?"

Spinning around on her feet, Koko stepped to her sister. "I'm not giving you shit! I helped take care of my nieces and nephew because that's what I wanted to do. I didn't bust nan nut when they were conceived therefore, I don't owe you shit. Daniyah, it's your fault you laid down on three different occasions and produced babies with nothing ass niggas. Should've done your research instead of opening your legs at every turn. Like I told your mother, the bank is closed. It's time for all of you muthafuckas to get the fuck off the pot and make something happen for yourselves. I did it! The shit was hard as fuck, but I went out and made a name for myself. Me! I did that without the help of any of you."

"Oh, so you get to be on the news broadcasting your talent and now you done forgot where you came from? Let me remind you. We're both from the southside of Chicago, raised by the same woman, and lived off welfare. You weren't always able to go into the store and not have to put anything back! You ate syrup sandwiches right along with the rest of us. Now you better than us?" Daniyah snarled.

"All that shit you just said was for what? Hell yeah, we grew up poor and was limited to things we could afford, but who said we had to continue to live that way? I wanted better and I went out to achieve it. Don't blame me for your lack of education and will to succeed. That's all on you. What you thought was money moves with these niggas were simply stupidity. See, I went out and hustled hard so I would never have to depend on another muthafucka to do a damn thing for me. I worked my ass off so I wouldn't have to beg anybody for shit! How does it feel to be the cum bucket your mother always talked to me about?"

Daniyah lunged at Koko because her words stung like a colony of bees. She was ready to fight her sister, but Kaz stepped between them. He noticed when Koko was upset, she didn't care what came out of her mouth. It was something she would have to work on because she was in a higher league than the streets of the southside. Kaz also understood when a person had enough of the bullshit she was going through. Family was the first to attempt to bring one down when they were on their way up.

"Bitch, don't act like you were never with child. Your ass was dumb for a nigga too! You're just mad your fucked up womb couldn't hold it."

Koko laughed at Daniyah's revelation of her past. "There is nothing you can say that will make me feel sorry for what happened to me. We are totally different in that department. I dodged a bullet; you were hit by three. Even if I had carried the baby full term, it would be well taken care of by me! You should take a few plays from me and maybe you'd be able to get out of the hole you're sinking further into. Go harass the bum ass niggas you call your baby daddies. You know, the ones that don't help you with shit because you can't help yourself."

"That's enough! This shit ain't going nowhere. Y'all out here putting each other's business in the street and what is it solving? Nothing. This is a meaningless argument," Kaz said turning directly to Daniyah. "I don't know you, but it would be wise for you to stay away from your sister. From my understanding, y'all wasn't there through the rough times but are always looking for a handout. It's not how shit works. Get ya bag up because your sister is done with all of you."

"Well, since you have so much to say, how about you give me the money."

Kaz shook his head and led Koko away. Daniyah was still talking shit, but the words Kaz said to Koko was the only reason she didn't double back to stomp a mudhole in her ass. She got to her truck and Horace and Alessia was standing in wait. Daniyah had one more thing to get off her chest and Koko paused to hear her out.

"I don't give a damn if I have to come to Minnesota, I'm whooping yo' ass, Kameeko!"

"Make sure you tell your mama where you're going so she can put out the missing person's report," Koko said before Kaz forced her into the driver's seat.

The days of her own flesh and blood strong arming her were over. Koko planned to fight to the very end to protect her peace. She would lay hands on whoever the fuck tried to get in her way. The life she was living was one she paved the way to enjoy. It was her against the world and she was ready for the battle.

Chapter 13

Cyrus hadn't heard from Koko since the night he saw her on the news. He called and texted her several times with no response. She wasn't back in Minnesota because he checked her studio and her apartment daily. He'd even sat in her place waiting for her to enter. That alone had Cyrus thinking about why Koko wasn't back home. His mind was on the fact of her being with the nigga she was so secretive about. There was no doubt in his mind…they were fucking.

He did some digging of his own and found out exactly who the nigga was. Kazimir St. Claire. A multimillionaire who owned his own business making candy. He learned that Kazimir inherited his wealth and never had to work hard for none of the shit he was being praised about. So what the muthafucka had been to college and was on his way to the NBA, but he didn't make it. In Cyrus' mind, Kazimir was a silver spoon baby that didn't know shit about the streets. That was the upper hand advantage he needed because he had plans to kill his lame ass.

"What are you thinking about?" Sheree asked. "You've been walking around with an attitude for days."

"Don't start this shit, Sheree."

"I just asked you a question, Cyrus."

"All in my damn business too. If I didn't tell you what's going on, then that means I won't. Go pack some clothes because I want you and Cj to come stay at my house with me."

Sheree stood with her hands on her hip. "Why do I have to come to an apartment when we can just stay here? It's cluttered over there because you use it like a damn warehouse."

"I have some business to take care of tonight. Have my son at my crib when I get there. You can leave after that. I'm out."

Cyrus left Sheree's and jumped in his whip heading to the trap. He was meeting with his team to prepare them for the meeting Lowkey was calling for the next day. Whoever the fuck was stealing would be handled. Cyrus wanted to make sure none of his workers had been anywhere near that particular trap. He didn't need any problems with missing money. He grabbed his phone as he sat at a red light.

"What up, Cyrus? Where you at? We here waiting on you."

"I'm on my way, Don. I was calling to make sure everybody was there."

"Is everything okay?"

"Yeah, but I'll go into detail when I get there in about fifteen minutes."

Ending the call, Cyrus hit the music on CarPlay and turned the volume up.

Look, I got homies in the ground, skeletons and bones
And niggas doin' life, they ain't never comin' home
They said I wouldn't make it or never see the throne
And my baby mama hate me 'cause she said I did her wrong
"Cause I left to chase my dreams, get it any means
I said that I'll be back, she wasn't listenin' to me
That back and forth arguin' was getting' in between
I said fuck them other niggas, I go get it with my team
If we all grind, we all shine, fuck a part-time
I used to play the block early mornin' and dark time
Now its G5 flight, fuck a depart time

It was hard times, nigga, now it's our time
Just take a look at my life, rappin' brought me back to life
'Cause I was in them streets, my heart was cold as a pack
of ice
Every night we strappin' like we was in Iraq to fight
'Cause niggas getting' murdered for a block that do a
stack a night

Listening to Meek rap had Cyrus thinking about how he was going to get back to life. He had Cj but that wasn't enough for him. Money wasn't the problem because Cyrus had that hand over fist. He just needed to figure out how he could make it last. That meant he would have to invest and get the fuck out of the streets. The bullshit of the dope game was something he wanted no parts of. Niggas were out there putting their hands in cookie jars that didn't belong to them. Cyrus didn't want to be associated with that type of shit because he would have to get blood on his hands in order to protect his family and himself.

For years he stayed out of shit and only had to put in work when necessary. Cyrus had a feeling that was about to change. As an organization, the people he worked with were sloppy as fuck. He trusted his team and that was far as it went. Cyrus had no clue who the Plug was and wish he did because he could easily drop some jewels on how they could improve and make more money. But first, he had to talk to his team. Cyrus pulled up to the trap and got out of his whip. As he walked up to the door, a regular walked up to him to cop some dope.

"Cyrus, what's up, man? I need something to hold me over. My pockets dry though."

"Ray, you know I'm not giving you shit on credit. I'on know why you even came over here on that bullshit."

"You know I'm good for it, brother."

"Nah, I don't," Cyrus said walking off.

"I know who's been hitting Lowkey spot," Ray said stopping him in his tracks. "Now, can I get something to hold me over?"

Cyrus gestured for Ray to come to him. When he was close enough, Cyrus yoked him off his feet by the neck. Struggling to get out of the grip Cyrus held strong, Ray clawed at his hands.

"Nigga, stop fuckin' scratchin' me!" he gritted, letting the dope fiend go. "Tell me what the fuck you know. I want you to know right now, if you lyin' I'm gon' permanently cure your addiction. In other words, I'm gon' kill yo' ass! Now talk!"

Ray shifted from foot to foot as he looked around for someone to save him from Cyrus' wrath. When he didn't see anyone, he started sweating profusely. The information he held could get him killed anyway, but Ray felt he would be safer under the protection of Cyrus. He also knew there was a possibility of him telling the truth and still lose his life. Ray couldn't win for losing.

"Look, it's some niggas from the north that Lowkey put on who has been skimming off the work they were given. They felt the money they were getting wasn't worth what they were rightfully due. So, they started hitting the stash at the trap when nobody was watching."

"My question to you is, why were they comfortable telling you what was going on, Ray?"

"Being a crackhead has its perks. Most times when muthafuckas think you're high, the ears are wide open. That's what happened a few weeks ago."

"How many people are involved in this shit?" Cyrus asked.

Ray was scratching his arms and neck viciously as he tried his best to stay focused on what he and Cyrus were discussing. The monkey was riding the fuck out of his back, and he needed a fix badly. Ray was trying to hold his composure, but he was losing the fight.

"Cyrus, can I please have some medicine first? I swear I'm gon' tell you all I know," Ray pled.

Cyrus took his phone from his pocket and called Don telling him to bring a five piece out front. It didn't take long for him to come out. Giving Ray a portion of his reward for snitching, Cyrus filled Don in on what he was told. He peeked over at Ray noticing the hunger in his eyes for the drug.

"Hit that bitch twice and not a puff more. You still got work to do. As a matter of fact, you will go with us to meet up with Lowkey."

"Nawl, Cyrus. I didn't agree to snitch on these niggas face to face. Do you know they will kill me over this shit? I'll talk to Lowkey, but I don't want nobody to know I'm the person who told." Ray all but cried. "Check this out, Jojo and Jerrod were the cats talking 'bout what they had done. They have stolen a lot of money and is out to get more since nobody has said anything about what they've already taken. That's all I have for you and that's on my life."

Ray laid it all out for Cyrus to take in and he couldn't believe Lowkey would put those bum ass niggas on. He could tell the person who put Lowkey in charge didn't do their homework on him because that nigga didn't do his. Sheree's people would bring the entire operation down if they were ever apprehended by the police. Cyrus heard all he needed to know. There was no reason for him to take Ray along for the ride.

"You can go, but don't get lost because you are now my informant. If you hear anything else, you come to me and me only. When I need you, I'll find you."

"I got you, Cyrus. You know where I live."

"Yes, I do. Remember what I said, Ray. Keep your mouth shut and keep moving the way you been."

Cyrus watched Ray scurry down the street. When he rounded the corner, he and Don went inside to chat with the team. The chatter came to an abrupt halt soon as the door opened, and Cyrus stepped inside. His ship was run with a closed fist even though he wasn't the big man in charge. He only wanted the best on the street to work beside him. The shit Ray told him had Cyrus shaking his head vigorously.

"Aye, as y'all know, there's some niggas with sticky fingers at the North trap. I just heard some fucked up shit, and I want to make sure none of my people is involved in the mess. Lowkey got his hands full with this one because of his actions. What I want to know is, if any of you niggas know anything about what's going on?"

The silence around the room was thick enough to cut with a knife. Nobody said anything and that caused Don and Cyrus to step further into the room like two beasts. One thing about Cyrus, he didn't like to repeat himself under any circumstance.

"If you know something, say something! This shit isn't considered snitching! It's called, if you bring this shit my way, you going down with the muthafucka responsible. I don't know if any of you niggas want those kind of problems from me. Now is not the time to be quiet; trust me."

One of his soldiers walked up and held his hands up. "I know it's those new niggas over there causing a lot of problems. I don't know shit about them stealing or no shit like that, but they've been stepping to the Somalians."

"When we get to that damn trap, you muthafuckas better talk. Lowkey ain't in the position to handle this shit. If things go my way, I'll be running both spots and that means more territory for us."

Looking over at Don, Cyrus was cool with what he said because it showed he was ready to take over whenever Cyrus decided to step down. If Jojo was fuckin' with the Somalians, that was more heat coming to Lowkey's ass. Those muthafuckas had gangs that was all about violence. Their murderous adventures were the ones that didn't make the media. But if they came with the bullshit, they were sure going to be on every mainstream platform if Cyrus had anything to do with it.

"We're about to head out. Don't just get there, beat me there."

Walking out of the trap, the whole crew was on his ass ready to roll out as Cyrus jumped in his whip. He pulled out and led the pack to their destination. The first thing he decided to do was call Koko. The phone rang, filling the interior of his vehicle. When the call went to voicemail, Cyrus called back.

"What do you want, Cyrus?" Koko answered with an attitude.

"Is that how you gon' talk to a nigga from now on?"

"I don't want to talk to your ass at all. You're on the verge of getting blocked to be honest. Cyrus, I want nothing to do with you and I wish you would get that through your head. It's over between us. It doesn't matter how much you text or call, after today, I won't answer."

"Koko, listen and listen good. No matter what we go through, you will belong to me forever. There is no getting out. I understand what I did was wrong, but I've apologized too many times. It's either you're going to forgive me, or you're just gonna deal with it. Cj is my son and there is nothing I can do to change the outcome. You and I can start our own family together. I promise I will love you like I've never done before."

The three beeps indicated the moment Koko ended the call. Her actions didn't do anything except piss him off. But once she gets home, he would hear from her because she couldn't go into her studio until she came to see him. Koko was going to learn there was no getting away from Cyrus Davis. He was lost in his thoughts and didn't realize he had arrived at the Northside trap. There were quite a few cars parked along the street, so Cyrus led his team to the vacant lot across the street.

As they exited their vehicles, Lowkey stood outside the gate of the backyard waiting to guide them inside. Cyrus could tell he was stressed from the dark circles around his eyes. Stepping to the side, Lowkey gestured everyone in. Cyrus glanced around at all the niggas in attendance while searching for Jojo and Jerrod. The thieving muthafuckas were nowhere in sight. He found a spot off to the side so he could hear exactly how Lowkey was going to handle the situation.

"I've waited far too long to bring this shit to y'all attention, and I regret that shit now. Every last one of y'all in this muthafucka eats good so tell me why money is disappearing at a rapid rate around here?" Lowkey asked looking around. "Don't everybody answer at once."

"Yo, Lowkey, we've been in this shit together for a while and nothing's been out of place. When did this shit start?" A young nigga named Shoota asked.

"Almost a month now." He said taking in the people around him.

"Tell me this," Shoota continued. "Where the new niggas at? Wasn't everybody supposed to be at this meeting? Correct me if I'm wrong."

Lowkey ran his hand down his face, and it seemed like he didn't know what to say. Cyrus moved in to help him out.

"At a time like this, yeah, everybody who works in this muthafucka should be here." Cyrus said turning his attention to the *man in charge*. "Tell me about these new niggas. What do you know about 'em?"

Lowkey looked perplexed before he shrugged. "They wanted to be put on and I did just that."

Cyrus eyebrow rose because he couldn't believe he'd done that dumb shit. In the profession they were in, not just anybody could be put on. Backgrounds needed to be checked. Niggas nowadays were working with the Feds or didn't know the first thing about hustling. Jojo and his cousin weren't informants; that Cyrus knew of. But they damn sure didn't know shit about handling drugs. All they wanted was fast money. Obviously, they accomplished what they set out to do.

"Word on the streets is you know the niggas." A tall lanky dude snarled at Cyrus. "More like family really."

"And who the fuck implemented me in y'all shit?" Cyrus snapped back. "Furthermore, I know muthafuckin' well you ain't insinuating I have something to do with the shortage."

"I mean, birds of a feather flock together. Jojo and Jerrod is yo' people!"

"See, just like I don't know you, nigga. You don't know shit about me. They just so happen to be related to my son, but I don't fuck with them niggas. A muthafucka like myself stand on my own bread. Taking from the next muthafucka is something I'm not with. Get yo' facts straight before you lose yo' life spreading false information."

"Is that a threat?" Dude asked, moving his hand to his hip.

Cyrus hated niggas who wanted to be tough. The niggas silently letting it be known he was strapped activated Cyrus' attack button. Before anyone knew what was occurring, Cyrus clothed lined his ass then followed him to the floor with his own tool in hand. Beating dude with the butt of his Glock, Cyrus didn't notice all the blood spewing from the side of his head until several hands pulled him off.

"Nigga, don't ever speak on me. Next time you won't get saved. I'm not the nigga to fuck wit! I'll kill yo' ass and pay for yo' muthafuckin' funeral!"

Cyrus was forced out of the trap. He shoved the niggas off him and tried to go back to finish what he started. Don prevented him from doing so by standing in front of him.

"Nah, brah. You already fucked that nigga up. I understand why you did it, but this is not our fight. Let's get out of here."

Cyrus was mad and wanted to fire into the trap when he saw dude stand to his feet through the window. Soon as he was about to follow his mind, the sound of a vehicle coming to a stop caught his and Don's attention. The Ashton Martin with dark tint had Cyrus wondering if the person inside was lost. It wasn't common for anybody in the hood to roll like that.

"Damn, that muthafucka nice!" One of Lowkey's groupies exclaimed. "Who is that?"

The driver emerged from the expensive vehicle with a phone to his ear. With his back turned, the waves were deep in his head and the cut was fresh. Cyrus forgot the Plug was coming through. The bullshit that happened inside the trap threw him off. He was disgusted by the way niggas lusted over a muthafucka with a nice whip. Ending the call he was on, the mystery man finally turned toward the trap, and another stepped out of the passenger's side.

Recognition clicked in Cyrus' mind and his rage was back full force. The nigga in the expensive suit was no other than Kazimir St. Clair. He knew damn well he wasn't the Plug and was there to holla at him about Koko. From the information Cyrus had gathered, the nigga owned a muthafuckin' candy company so he didn't know shit about the streets. Lowkey came out of the trap nervously forcing a smile as he made his way down the walkway.

"Kaz, what's up? Steelo, it's been a minute. I didn't know you were coming too."

"You already know I'm wherever I need to be when it comes to this one. Anyway, what's the deal? Tell us what's going on."

"Well, I found out who may have taken the money."

"Okay, where are they?" Kaz asked glancing in the direction Cyrus and the others were standing. "Are these the ones involved?"

"Hell nawl, we not involved," Cyrus barked.

"And you are?"

"None of yo' business. I don't work out of this trap, but I've been called to this muthafucka because of their fuck up. Who are you?"

Kaz didn't like the disrespect that was thrown at him. He didn't come all the way to Minnesota to make an example out of a muthafucka but he had no problem doing so. The nigga glaring at him did what most people in the past had done, and that was judge him by his attire. Kaz decided to keep shit professional for the time being before things got ugly.

"Let's start over. I'm Kaz, and you are?"

"I know who you are. The question is, why are you worried about street shit?"

"Come on, Cyrus. You overstepping right now. Have some respect."

Cyrus eyebrows furrowed as he stepped to Lowkey. "How the fuck can I have respect for niggas that can't run an organization. Yo' ass riding a dick of a muthafucka who knows nothing about what we do out here in these streets. Is it because he got money?"

Kaz chortled because he couldn't believe someone so arrogant was on his team. It was obvious Cyrus knew something about him, and it had to be the public record of Kaz being an entrepreneur. What he didn't know was that he also ran the entire Midwest. Kaz loved a cocky nigga and he was about to learn to put money behind his research; he would've found out more than he thought about him.

"Cyrus, is it?" Kaz asked rubbing his manicured hands together. "What makes you think I don't have knowledge of the streets?"

"Far as I know, you're the candy man in Chicago. A silver spoon baby is what you muthafuckas are called. You push sweet candy. I push that bugga suga. We ain't the same. On top of that, you like to mess around with women that don't belong to you," Cyrus snarled.

Kaz didn't know what the Cyrus dude was insinuating, but he had time to hear him out. It was his first encounter with the cat, and he had no clue who or what he was referring to. Cyrus was serious about what he said so, there had to be

196

some type of validation in his words. Kaz's silence had him thinking he hit the nail on the head because Cyrus went on to explain.

"I heard about what happened at Reign with my girl and how you saved the hoe. At the time, I didn't know who the fuck you were until I saw you on T.V. with her ass. In case you still want to play dumb, her name is Kameeko Simmons. Yeah, that's my bitch."

Kaz shook his head because Cyrus was in his feelings about a woman he constantly disrespected and had her acting out in public behind his bullshit. He wasn't going to speak on what they had going on because he didn't know the details. Koko was woman enough not to even mention her ex's name when she talked about her situation. But Kaz was ready to get down to the root of his missing money.

"Whatever you have going on with the young lady you're speaking on, that's between y'all. I'm here to discuss business."

"Nawl, we're about to discuss Koko! You don't have a hand in this business so nothing about that will be passed on to you. Call the boss and tell him to come through. We not talking to a flunky."

Kaz was over the disrespect. He grabbed Cyrus by the throat squeezing his fingers together tightly. "I am the muthafuckin' Boss, nigga," he gritted. "Your emotions about a female clouded the fuck out of your judgement. Yes, I am the man you saw on T.V. with Kameeko, but she's not a hoe, nor anyone's bitch! She is a woman going places and she can't do that shit with a muthafucka who works the block while slinging dick to whomever allows you to put that shit between their legs." Pushing Cyrus away, Kaz seethed with anger. "So, there's no confusion, you work for me! I'm the muthafuckin' plug and I want to know where the fuck my money is. You say this isn't the spot you work out of, then this shit doesn't concern you."

"But Koko concerns me, nigga!" Cyrus shot back. "Stay the fuck away from her!"

Kaz laughed. "Yo' soft ass is dismissed. You are no longer needed at this meeting."

Cyrus reached for his tool, but Don once again stopped him. He knew firsthand who Kaz was and he was going to fill his boy in on that shit. Beef with that nigga was something Cyrus didn't want. Kaz was a deadly nigga if pushed to the limit. Whatever was going on with him and Koko, Cyrus needed to push it to the side. His entire livelihood was in the palm of that man's hand. As Don guided Cyrus to his whip, Kaz's voice sent a shiver down his spine.

"Take a few days off from working. I'll have somebody run your shit until I decide if you continue to eat or not. The way you pop yo' shit, you sound like you set either way. I'll be in touch."

Don pushed Cyrus into the passenger seat of the car and hurried to the driver's side. Driving off, Cyrus was cursing and calling Koko every name in the book. Seeing Kaz really did something to him after learning he was connected to what he considered his woman.

"Drive back around. I'm about to kill this muthafucka!"

"Nawl, man. It ain't even worth it."

Cyrus pulled his Glock, aiming it at Don's head. "I said drive back around, nigga!"

Shooting Don was something Cyrus wouldn't do but he didn't know that. All he wanted was for him to get back on the block so he could handle his business. There was no way Kaz was going to take his woman and smile in his face like he was a fuckin' joke.

In the short amount of time Cyrus pulled off, Kaz learned the names of the people involved in taking his money. He informed Lowkey about his plans to replace him. Lowkey didn't like what he heard but he had to respect it. His main concern was running his club anyway so it wasn't like he didn't have an income to fall back on. He fucked up and had to deal with the consequences. Lowkey would take getting fired over being slumped because three hundred thousand was a lot of money for one to lose.

Kurt, the nigga Cyrus pistol-whipped, came out of the trap bloody as hell. He informed Kaz about Cyrus' relation to the people that stole from them. He opened his mouth to address Lowkey about withholding information when the sound of screeching tires caught their attention. Bullets clattered around them causing everyone to pull their weapons while trying to find shelter. The vehicle zoomed down the street and the silence were deafening.

When the smoke cleared, Kurt was riddled with bullets, and Kaz was lying motionless on the pavement. Lowkey and Steelo ran to check him out. Blood slid from Kaz's mouth, and he was struggling to breathe. A red spot formed on the right side of his dress shirt.

"Help me get him to the car! I need to get him to the hospital," Steelo yelled.

When they got Kaz in the back of the car, he closed his eyes, but his chest rose and fell slowly. Steelo hopped behind the wheel and sped away to the nearest hospital. He couldn't lose his best friend to this street shit. He had too much going on and the nigga Cyrus was going to get what's coming to him for what he had done.

To be continued...

Click the link to Follow Me on all social media platforms and also to download many more of my books.
https://linktr.ee/authormeesha

Lock Down Publications and Ca$h Presents
Assisted Publishing Packages

BASIC PACKAGE $499 Editing Cover Design Formatting	**UPGRADED PACKAGE** $800 Typing Editing Cover Design Formatting
ADVANCE PACKAGE $1,200 Typing Editing Cover Design Formatting Copyright registration Proofreading Upload book to Amazon	**LDP SUPREME PACKAGE** $1,500 Typing Editing Cover Design Formatting Copyright registration Proofreading Set up Amazon account Upload book to Amazon Advertise on LDP, Amazon and Facebook Page

***Other services available upon request.
Additional charges may apply

Lock Down Publications
P.O. Box 944
Stockbridge, GA 30281-9998
Phone: 470 303-9761

Submission Guideline

Submit the first three chapters of your completed manuscript to ldpsubmissions@gmail.com. In the subject line add **Your Book's Title**. The manuscript must be in a Word Doc file and sent as an attachment. Document should be in Times New Roman, double spaced, and in size 12 font. Also, provide your synopsis and full contact information. If sending multiple submissions, they must each be in a separate email.

Have a story but no way to send it electronically? You can still submit to LDP/Ca$h Presents. Send in the first three chapters, written or typed, of your completed manuscript to:

LDP: Submissions Dept
P.O. Box 944
Stockbridge, GA 30281-9998

DO NOT send original manuscript. Must be a duplicate.
Provide your synopsis and a cover letter containing your full contact information.

Thanks for considering LDP and Ca$h Presents.

NEW RELEASES

BLOODLINE OF A SAVAGE 1&2
THESE VICIOUS STREETS 1&2
RELENTLESS GOON
RELENTLESS GOON 2
BY PRINCE A. TAUHID

THE BUTTERFLY MAFIA 1-3
BY FUMIYA PAYNE

A THUG'S STREET PRINCESS 1&2
BY MEESHA

CITY OF SMOKE 2
BY MOLOTTI

STEPPERS 1,2&3
THE REAL BADDIES OF CHI-RAQ
BY KING RIO

THE LANE 1&2
BY KEN-KEN SPENCE

THUG OF SPADES 1&2
LOVE IN THE TRENCHES 2
CORNER BOYS
BY COREY ROBINSON

TIL DEATH 3
BY ARYANNA

THE BIRTH OF A GANGSTER 4
BY DELMONT PLAYER

PRODUCT OF THE STREETS 1&2
BY DEMOND "MONEY" ANDERSON

NO TIME FOR ERROR
BY KEESE

MONEY HUNGRY DEMONS
BY TRANAY ADAMS

Coming Soon from Lock Down Publications/Ca$h Presents

IF YOU CROSS ME ONCE 6
ANGEL V
By Anthony Fields

IMMA DIE BOUT MINE 5
By Aryanna

A THUGS STREET PRINCESS 3
By Meesha

PRODUCT OF THE STREETS 3
By Demond Money Anderson

CORNER BOYS 2
By Corey Robinson

THE MURDER QUEENS 6&7
By Michael Gallon

CITY OF SMOKE 3
By Molotti

CONFESSIONS OF A DOPE BOY
By Nicholas Lock

THA TAKEOVER
By Keith Chandler

BETRAYAL OF A G 2
By Ray Vinci

CRIME BOSS
By Playa Ray

Available Now

RESTRAINING ORDER 1 & 2
By **CA$H & Coffee**

LOVE KNOWS NO BOUNDARIES 1-3
By **Coffee**

RAISED AS A GOON I, II, III & IV
BRED BY THE SLUMS I, II, III
BLAST FOR ME I & II
ROTTEN TO THE CORE I II III
A BRONX TALE I, II, III
DUFFLE BAG CARTEL I II III IV V VI
HEARTLESS GOON I II III IV V
A SAVAGE DOPEBOY I II
DRUG LORDS I II III
CUTTHROAT MAFIA I II
KING OF THE TRENCHES
By **Ghost**

LAY IT DOWN I & II
LAST OF A DYING BREED I II
BLOOD STAINS OF A SHOTTA I & II III
By **Jamaica**

LOYAL TO THE GAME I II III
LIFE OF SIN I, II III
By **TJ & Jelissa**

IF LOVING HIM IS WRONG...I & II
LOVE ME EVEN WHEN IT HURTS I II III
By **Jelissa**

PUSH IT TO THE LIMIT
By **Bre' Hayes**

BLOODY COMMAS I & II
SKI MASK CARTEL I, II & III
KING OF NEW YORK I II, III IV V
RISE TO POWER I II III
COKE KINGS I II III IV V
BORN HEARTLESS I II III IV
KING OF THE TRAP I II
By **T.J. Edwards**

WHEN THE STREETS CLAP BACK I & II III
THE HEART OF A SAVAGE I II III IV
MONEY MAFIA I II
LOYAL TO THE SOIL I II III
By **Jibril Williams**

A DISTINGUISHED THUG STOLE MY HEART I II & III
LOVE SHOULDN'T HURT I II III IV
RENEGADE BOYS 1-4
PAID IN KARMA 1-3
SAVAGE STORMS 1-3
AN UNFORESEEN LOVE 1-3
BABY, I'M WINTERTIME COLD 1-3
A THUG'S STREET PRINCESS 1&2
By **Meesha**

A GANGSTER'S CODE 1-3
A GANGSTER'S SYN 1-3
THE SAVAGE LIFE 1-3
CHAINED TO THE STREETS 1-3
BLOOD ON THE MONEY 1-3
A GANGSTA'S PAIN 1-3
BEAUTIFUL LIES AND UGLY TRUTHS
CHURCH IN THESE STREETS
By **J-Blunt**

CUM FOR ME 1-8
An LDP Erotica Collaboration

BLOOD OF A BOSS 1-5
SHADOWS OF THE GAME
TRAP BASTARD
By **Askari**

THE STREETS BLEED MURDER 1-3
THE HEART OF A GANGSTA 1-3
By **Jerry Jackson**

WHEN A GOOD GIRL GOES BAD
By **Adrienne**

THE COST OF LOYALTY 1-3
By **Kweli**

BRIDE OF A HUSTLA 1-3
THE FETTI GIRLS 1-3
CORRUPTED BY A GANGSTA 1-4
BLINDED BY HIS LOVE
THE PRICE YOU PAY FOR LOVE 1-3
DOPE GIRL MAGIC 1-3
By **Destiny Skai**

A KINGPIN'S AMBITION
A KINGPIN'S AMBITION II
I MURDER FOR THE DOUGH
By **Ambitious**

TRUE SAVAGE 1-7
DOPE BOY MAGIC 1-3
MIDNIGHT CARTEL 1-3
CITY OF KINGZ 1&2
NIGHTMARE ON SILENT AVE
THE PLUG OF LIL MEXICO 1&2
CLASSIC CITY
By **Chris Green**

A GANGSTER'S REVENGE 1-4
THE BOSS MAN'S DAUGHTERS 1-5
A SAVAGE LOVE 1&2
BAE BELONGS TO ME 1&2
A HUSTLER'S DECEIT 1-3
WHAT BAD BITCHES DO 1-3
SOUL OF A MONSTER 1-3
KILL ZONE
A DOPE BOY'S QUEEN 1-3
TIL DEATH 1-3
IMMA DIE BOUT MINE 1-4
By **Aryanna**

A DOPEBOY'S PRAYER
By **Eddie "Wolf" Lee**

THE KING CARTEL 1-3
By **Frank Gresham**

THESE NIGGAS AIN'T LOYAL 1-3
By **Nikki Tee**

GANGSTA SHYT 1-3
By **CATO**

THE ULTIMATE BETRAYAL
By **Phoenix**

BOSS'N UP 1-3
By **Royal Nicole**

I LOVE YOU TO DEATH
By **Destiny J**

I RIDE FOR MY HITTA
I STILL RIDE FOR MY HITTA
By **Misty Holt**

LOVE & CHASIN' PAPER
By **Qay Crockett**

TO DIE IN VAIN
SINS OF A HUSTLA
By **ASAD**

BROOKLYN HUSTLAZ
By **Boogsy Morina**

BROOKLYN ON LOCK 1 & 2
By **Sonovia**

GANGSTA CITY
By **Teddy Duke**

A DRUG KING AND HIS DIAMOND 1-3
A DOPEMAN'S RICHES
HER MAN, MINE'S TOO 1&2
CASH MONEY HO'S
THE WIFEY I USED TO BE 1&2
PRETTY GIRLS DO NASTY THINGS
By **Nicole Goosby**

LIPSTICK KILLAH 1-3
CRIME OF PASSION 1-3
FRIEND OR FOE 1-3
By **Mimi**

TRAPHOUSE KING 1-3
KINGPIN KILLAZ 1-3
STREET KINGS 1&2
PAID IN BLOOD 1&2
CARTEL KILLAZ 1-3
DOPE GODS 1&2
By **Hood Rich**

THE STREETS ARE CALLING
By **Duquie Wilson**

STEADY MOBBN' 1-3
THE STREETS STAINED MY SOUL 1-3
By **Marcellus Allen**

WHO SHOT YA 1-3
SON OF A DOPE FIEND 1-4
HEAVEN GOT A GHETTO 1&2
SKI MASK MONEY 1&2
By **Renta**

GORILLAZ IN THE BAY 1-4
TEARS OF A GANGSTA 1/&2
3X KRAZY 1&2
STRAIGHT BEAST MODE 1&2
By **DE'KARI**

TRIGGADALE 1-3
MURDA WAS THE CASE 1-3
By **Elijah R. Freeman**

SLAUGHTER GANG 1-3
RUTHLESS HEART 1-3
By **Willie Slaughter**

GOD BLESS THE TRAPPERS 1-3
THESE SCANDALOUS STREETS 1-3
FEAR MY GANGSTA 1-5
THESE STREETS DON'T LOVE NOBODY 1-2
BURY ME A G 1-5
A GANGSTA'S EMPIRE 1-4
THE DOPEMAN'S BODYGAURD 1&2
THE REALEST KILLAZ 1-3
THE LAST OF THE OGS 1-3
By **Tranay Adams**

MARRIED TO A BOSS 1-3
By **Destiny Skai & Chris Green**

KINGZ OF THE GAME 1-7
CRIME BOSS 1-3
By **Playa Ray**

FUK SHYT
By **Blakk Diamond**

DON'T F#CK WITH MY HEART 1&2
By **Linnea**

ADDICTED TO THE DRAMA 1-3
IN THE ARM OF HIS BOSS
By **Jamila**

LOYALTY AIN'T PROMISED 1&2
By **Keith Williams**

YAYO 1-4
A SHOOTER'S AMBITION 1&2
BRED IN THE GAME
By **S. Allen**

TRAP GOD 1-3
RICH $AVAGE 1-3
MONEY IN THE GRAVE 1-3
CARTEL MONEY
By **Martell Troublesome Bolden**

FOREVER GANGSTA 1&2
GLOCKS ON SATIN SHEETS 1&2
By **Adrian Dulan**

TOE TAGZ 1-4
LEVELS TO THIS SHYT 1&2
IT'S JUST ME AND YOU
By **Ah'Million**

KINGPIN DREAMS 1-3
RAN OFF ON DA PLUG
By **Paper Boi Rari**

THE STREETS MADE ME 1-3
By **Larry D. Wright**

CONFESSIONS OF A GANGSTA 1-4
CONFESSIONS OF A JACKBOY 1-3
CONFESSIONS OF A HITMAN
By **Nicholas Lock**

I'M NOTHING WITHOUT HIS LOVE
SINS OF A THUG
TO THE THUG I LOVED BEFORE
A GANGSTA SAVED XMAS
IN A HUSTLER I TRUST
By **Monet Dragun**

QUIET MONEY 1-3
THUG LIFE 1-3
EXTENDED CLIP 1&2
A GANGSTA'S PARADISE
By **Trai'Quan**

CAUGHT UP IN THE LIFE 1-3
THE STREETS NEVER LET GO 1-3
By **Robert Baptiste**

NEW TO THE GAME 1-3
MONEY, MURDER & MEMORIES 1-3
By **Malik D. Rice**

CREAM 2-3
THE STREETS WILL TALK
By **Yolanda Moore**

THE STREETS WILL NEVER CLOSE 1-3
By **K'ajji**

LIFE OF A SAVAGE 1-4
A GANGSTA'S QUR'AN 1-4
MURDA SEASON 1-3
GANGLAND CARTEL 1-3
CHI'RAQ GANGSTAS 1-4
KILLERS ON ELM STREET 1-3
JACK BOYZ N DA BRONX 1-3
A DOPEBOY'S DREAM 1-3
JACK BOYS VS DOPE BOYS 1-3
COKE GIRLZ
COKE BOYS
SOSA GANG 1&2
BRONX SAVAGES
BODYMORE KINGPINS
BLOOD OF A GOON
By **Romell Tukes**

CONCRETE KILLA 1-3
VICIOUS LOYALTY 1-3
By **Kingpen**

THE ULTIMATE SACRIFICE 1-6
KHADIFI
IF YOU CROSS ME ONCE 1-3
ANGEL 1-4
IN THE BLINK OF AN EYE
By **Anthony Fields**

THE LIFE OF A HOOD STAR
By **Ca$h & Rashia Wilson**

NIGHTMARES OF A HUSTLA 1-3
BLOOD AND GAMES 1&2
By **King Dream**

GHOST MOB
By **Stilloan Robinson**

HARD AND RUTHLESS 1&2
MOB TOWN 251
THE BILLIONAIRE BENTLEYS 1-3
REAL G'S MOVE IN SILENCE
By **Von Diesel**

MOB TIES 1-7
SOUL OF A HUSTLER, HEART OF A KILLER 1-3
GORILLAZ IN THE TRENCHES
By **SayNoMore**

BODYMORE MURDERLAND 1-3
THE BIRTH OF A GANGSTER 1-4
By **Delmont Player**

FOR THE LOVE OF A BOSS 1&2
By **C. D. Blue**

KILLA KOUNTY 1-5
By **Khufu**

MOBBED UP 1-4
THE BRICK MAN 1-5
THE COCAINE PRINCESS 1-10
STEPPERS 1-3
SUPER GREMLIN 1-4
By **King Rio**

MONEY GAME 1&2
By **Smoove Dolla**

A GANGSTA'S KARMA 1-4
By **FLAME**

KING OF THE TRENCHES 1-3
By **GHOST & TRANAY ADAMS**

QUEEN OF THE ZOO 1&2
By **Black Migo**

GRIMEY WAYS 1-3
BETRAYAL OF A G
By **Ray Vinci**

XMAS WITH AN ATL SHOOTER
By **Ca$h & Destiny Skai**

KING KILLA 1&2
By **Vincent "Vitto" Holloway**

BETRAYAL OF A THUG 1&2
By **Fre$h**

THE MURDER QUEENS 1-5
By **Michael Gallon**

FOR THE LOVE OF BLOOD 1-4
By **Jamel Mitchell**

HOOD CONSIGLIERE 1&2
NO TIME FOR ERROR
By **Keese**

PROTÉGÉ OF A LEGEND 1&2
LOVE IN THE TRENCHES 1&2
By **Corey Robinson**

THE PLUG'S RUTHLESS DAUGHTER
By **Tony Daniels**

BORN IN THE GRAVE 1-3
CRIME PAYS
By **Self Made Tay**

MOAN IN MY MOUTH
By **XTASY**

TORN BETWEEN A GANGSTER AND A GENTLEMAN
By **J-BLUNT & Miss Kim**

LOYALTY IS EVERYTHING 1-3
CITY OF SMOKE 1&2
By **Molotti**

HERE TODAY GONE TOMORROW 1&2
By **Fly Rock**

WOMEN LIE MEN LIE 1-4
FIFTY SHADES OF SNOW 1-3
STACK BEFORE YOU SPLURGE
GIRLS FALL LIKE DOMINOES
NAÏVE TO THE STREETS
By **ROY MILLIGAN**

PILLOW PRINCESS
By **S. Hawkins**

THE BUTTERFLY MAFIA 1-3
SALUTE MY SAVAGERY 1&2
By **Fumiya Payne**

THE LANE 1&2
By Ken-Ken Spence

THE PUSSY TRAP 1-5
By **Nene Capri**

DIRTY DNA
By **Blaque**

SANCTIFIED AND HORNY
by **XTASY**

BOOKS BY LDP'S CEO, CA$H

TRUST IN NO MAN
TRUST IN NO MAN 2
TRUST IN NO MAN 3
BONDED BY BLOOD
SHORTY GOT A THUG
THUGS CRY
THUGS CRY 2
THUGS CRY 3
TRUST NO BITCH
TRUST NO BITCH 2
TRUST NO BITCH 3
TIL MY CASKET DROPS
RESTRAINING ORDER
RESTRAINING ORDER 2
IN LOVE WITH A CONVICT
LIFE OF A HOOD STAR
XMAS WITH AN ATL SHOOTER

www.ingramcontent.com/pod-product-compliance
Lightning Source LLC
Chambersburg PA
CBHW071156260626
47162CB00003B/1077